KNOCK DOWN
DRAGON OUT

KNOCK DOWN DRAGON OUT

SOULMATE SHIFTERS IN MYSTERY, ALASKA
BOOK ONE

KRYSTAL SHANNAN

Published by KS Publishing

Cover by Clarise Tan of CT Cover Creations
Dragon Illustration by John Molinero
Formatting by Kate Tilton's Author Services, LLC (www.katetilton.com)

ACKNOWLEDGMENTS

This book, ya'll. I just can't tell you how excited I am for you to be reading it. For it to finally be ready. The past year was a rough one, but I feel like this book is getting me on my feet again. I can't wait for you to fall in love with Col and Naomi, and Kann, and Tor, and Saul and all the others of the Tribe in Mystery. I absolutely fell in love with these characters. I've cried with them. I've laughed with them. And now it's your turn. It's a whole new world. Soulmate Shifters is completely separate from any of my previous books. I hope you are ready for an adventure.

Thank you Becca for sticking with me through everything. In the words of Meredith Grey, "You're my person." I don't think I couldn't gotten through the last half of 2017 without you and Verity pushing me through. You helped make this new series a reality and I still can't believe that at the very beginning we thought Owen's book was first. WHEW! So glad we caught that. It just wouldn't have been the same without Col in the lead.

Thank you hubby for letting me spend so many hours in front of a laptop and always telling me to go after my dreams. Well, that and to 'take over the world'. LOL. I love you so much.

Thank you to my alpha reader Shelane! Girl, we had so much fun with this book and I wouldn't have caught everything without you asking questions and pushing me to take it further.

Huge shout out and hugs to my editor Chrissy, Shelane, and Tammy! And my beta readers, Kathleen, Iris, Krystal, Hannah, Sheila, and Laurie. I think I'm forgetting someone, so if you're name's not on the list, I apologize.

And to my readers, the biggest thanks to you. Without your support I wouldn't be where I am today. I wouldn't be able to write and create. Thank you for being Team Krystal Shannan.

Hugs,
Krystal

"I would not wish any companion in the world but you"

— WILLIAM SHAKESPEARE

CHAPTER
ONE

COL

Flaming rocks from erupting volcanoes seared Col's sides as he tucked his dragon wings tight and dove through the air. He chased the fleeing traitors from his world into a new one—an unknown one—through the portal horizon that shimmered like liquid magick.

His wings pumped hard. Anger surged through his veins, spurring him on. *Kill. Kill. Kill.* His dragon chanted inside his head. *They* had taken everything.

He would take it back.

The two remaining dragons who'd murdered the House of Li'Vhram would die an excruciating and painful death. Soon he'd be able to sink his talons into their flesh and rip them to shreds. Soon, his family's deaths would be avenged. Soon justice would be served.

Fire was coming to claim their souls.

His fire.

The intense heat of Reylea's burning air disappeared as he broke through the surface of the portal into unfamiliar blue skies. A blast of bitter cold wind made him blink hard. The land around him was white, and the sun reflected off the surface, blinding him.

He pumped his wings, struggling to adjust to a new gravity. His body dropped, smashing through the trees to the ground below. He thrashed about until he was finally upright and on all four of his claws.

The wind was numbingly cold with a scent on the air he didn't recognize. Reylea, his home, was all jungle and desert. It was never cold. Never like this... He raised a claw and looked down at the large print it'd made in the white powder coating the ground. He sniffed and licked it, surprised to find that it melted to water on his tongue.

He walked forward from the trees into a large clearing on the side of a hill. Jagged peaks rose around him on three sides. He squinted at the strange brightness. Movement caught his eye to his left. A bugle call of a dragon hunting cut through the air a moment later.

They'd been in this new world only a few minutes. What could the traitors possibly have found to hunt?

A scream broke the silence next.

A woman.

Col bounded forward a few steps and launched himself into the air.

He pumped his wings, climbing into the sky, and dipped toward the sound of shouts and another scream. Then came the sickening thud of a body slamming against something hard. Had they killed someone? He dove to the ground, shifting just as his claws touched the white powder. Feet replaced claws. He ran forward, through the trees tracking by scent, even in his human form. The two dragons had shifted as well.

The strong scent of the trees burned at his nostrils like the medicine the healers of Reylea used to treat lung sickness.

"Now you've broken her," a female voice screeched through the silence of the woods, like the scream of a panther, sharp and cold and heartless.

Col slowed his run, careful to pick through the trees without sounding like a bellowing river cow.

"She's just knocked unconscious. She will wake."

"Her head bleeds," the female voice spoke again, this time more annoyed than angry. "Col was right behind us. We need to get away from the portal. He could come through at any moment. She can tell us nothing about this world. This female is of no use anymore."

"Neither are you, sister." The male's voice was dark and angry, brewing like a summer storm on the horizon.

The female scoffed but didn't argue further.

Col crept around a small cluster of trees with green needles clinging to their branches. The cold white powder had weighed them down, so they almost touched the ground, providing him with excellent cover. With the element of surprise on his side, taking down the two traitors wouldn't be a challenge.

Kill. His dragon whispered inside his head. *They deserve to die.*

He peered around the last tree in the clump. The female—Sefa—was leaning against the trunk of a tall tree looking bored, while her brother, Jaha was crouched over a bundled-up form on the ground, likely the injured female they'd been speaking about.

Col's lip curled as fury built in his blood. Like the volcanoes erupting and destroying his home world, he was ready to boil and burn these two for their part in murdering his family.

His whole tribe.

He leapt forward as Jaha started to lift the injured woman from the ground. Col shifted to dragon form in mid-leap, knocking the traitor away from the woman with a roar.

Jaha shifted before Col could bite down, but he got a good slice at the other dragon's stomach before he tore loose from Col's grip. He pumped his wings, following Jaha high into the sky.

Another cry from below made him shift direction quickly. The female dragon had joined the fray, and shot through the air, missing him by inches. He banked a sharp turn and came face to face with both of them. This was it. This was the moment he would deliver justice for their crimes.

They would die.

Col dove at Jaha first since he was already bleeding. The female was smaller and less of a threat anyway. Jaha turned, protecting his stomach, but Col got in a good bite on his back, ripping off several armored spikes in the process.

He trumpeted into the sky and backed off just as the female came at him. Col turned and swatted her away with a well-trained swipe of his spiked tail.

Sefa fell, landing in the white powder near the woman on the ground.

He'd been trained by the royal guard and was one of the best warriors of his house. These two didn't have a chance ... and yet they kept coming at him. They knew they would die. He could see the fear in their wide-slitted eyes and hear the way their heartbeats raced in their chests.

Sefa swatted the blue bundled body across the clearing angrily before leaping back into the air.

Col shouldn't care. Shouldn't have looked. But he saw it, and there was no going back. The woman was glowing. Her soul. It was calling to him. Every part of him seized in that moment. His heart stopped. His lungs froze. His skin tightened.

Mate.

He gulped for a breath of the cold air and ducked another hit from Jaha, sending the lesser dragon careening into the trees. Sefa tried for a hit too, but he sent her flailing off through the sky with a solid blow to her chest.

He roared, bellowing a call across the sky. Both of them trumpeted back, but instead of charging, they swooped down and fled, flying just above the canopy of white-covered trees.

Col puffed out a breath of fire after their retreating figures. Nothing would slake his fury but their deaths.

Damn Fate.

But he wouldn't abandon his mate. Not even for those two traitors.

This world was cold, and the scents burned his

nostrils. He peered back over his shoulder. The portal was lower than it'd been earlier. The magick-bender must've realized she would send most of the Reyleans tumbling to their deaths if it weren't adjusted. Not everyone had the body of a dragon that could absorb a fall like he had.

The scent of fresh blood drew all his attention back to the woman on the ground. She was so small and defenseless. Even now, some predator could be stalking her helpless form. He'd find a shelter to hide her in. Keep her safe and well fed. Then he'd hunt down Sefa and Jaha. Their deaths wouldn't be today, but they would be soon.

Col flew back to the ground, landing softly and shifting. The transformation from his animal form to his two-legged version was as seamless as breathing. He ran across the clearing, toward the place where the woman had been.

Broken trees littered the way back. She was still there. Her light blue covering rose and fell with each breath. He could hear the strength in her heartbeat. She was a fighter.

Mate. His dragon growled from inside his chest.

She lay face down on the ground. Helpless. Unconscious.

Why now? Why would Fate choose this moment to give me a mate?

Col lifted her gently from the ground. He carried her beneath the shelter of one of the taller trees. One glance at her face and all thoughts of vengeance melted away, filling his heart with a love he'd never experienced before.

The muscles in his arms trembled, and his dragon preened. He placed her flat on the snowy ground. Her skin was the color of desert sand. Gorgeous and smooth. Her curls were wild and created a shining halo around her face. But breathtaking beauty wasn't what had his heart kicking the inside of his ribcage. He'd seen her glow—the *soul call*—from the air. Felt its pull. Yet, it was so much *more* up close.

Her skin was luminescent, like she'd swallowed active magick and it was trying to escape but couldn't. Like she carried a living flame of white light within her. It was beautiful and alluring and...

Mine.

No. It couldn't be. He couldn't have a mate in this strange world.

He was here for vengeance. In all his years, Fate had never seen fit to give him a mate. He'd had women in his bed from time to time, but never a mate. Never a woman who could give him more than a few moments of meaningless pleasure.

Mine. His dragon repeated. *Take her.*

Col huffed out a growl and turned to walk away but couldn't. The magick of the *soul call* was strong. He couldn't just leave her here either. Wild animals would find her. Whatever predators lived in this wilderness would be dangerous.

Nothing so soft could survive this bitter cold, which begged the question as to why this small slip of a female was out here all alone. Was she running from something? Had someone abandoned her already? Fire warmed his belly at the thought of someone hurting or mistreating his mate.

He glanced down at his hands. The left was stained with blood that wasn't his. The scent was different. His attention locked in on the female again. She was injured, and he was doing *nothing*.

Col ripped a strip of purple fabric from the swath tied around his waist. The leather strips hanging from his wide belt flapped against his legs in the cold wind. His dragon was making up for the temperature change, keeping his core warm, but it didn't make the bite of the wind any less uncomfortable. His entire torso was bare and feeling the discomfort of this new world's environment.

He pulled back the woman's hood, surprised to find that her hair was shorter than his, barely hanging past her ears in silky brown spirals. The wound was on the back of her head, near the base. It wasn't deep enough to need to be cauterized or sewn.

Col fastened the fabric, wrapping it twice around her head before tying it tightly. The bleeding wasn't flowing too strongly. He'd bandaged enough wounds to know hers would stop soon now that it was dressed.

Her face was exquisite. Even though he couldn't see her eyes, she had strong lines and a mouth that he wanted to explore. There was something about her scent ... almost like she was in heat. Like her very essence called to him. He leaned closer and sniffed her neck, breathing in the sweet fragrance of her.

Mine. His dragon rumbled again.

"Yes," he assured his inner beast. He was keeping her.

He was just going to find a safe place to hide her for a while and then continue after the two traitors—Jaha and his sister. He had a mission.

He was stronger than Fate's call. He could resist the beautiful mate Fate had placed in front of him ... for a while. It was a test of his will. Nothing more.

CHAPTER
TWO

COL

Col shifted back to dragon form and carefully picked up the injured woman in his large claws.

Mate. Mine, his dragon thought, pleased they were taking her with them.

He tucked her safely against his chest and heaved himself into the clear blue skies with a powerful flap of his wings. It took a moment to get high enough to catch the wind stream, but soon he was soaring over the wilderness below.

Herds of tasty looking creatures roamed below. Swaths of white powder covered the trees and mountains. It was beautiful ... in a strange, new way. He wasn't completely opposed to the cold. It was just different than Reylea's eternal warmth.

He swooped lower, trailing the herd of running deer-like creatures. They'd seen his shadow approach and fled but were no match for his speed. Col dipped his head low enough to snatch a large one right from the back of the running herd.

Two snaps of his powerful jaws and the snack was gone. His belly was full, and he pumped his wings harder, thrusting himself back upward, high into the wind-stream. He caught the powerful current of air and let his wings billow like the sails of a ship.

The scent of the traitors was powerful in the air, but he kept his eyes looking for a village or camp of some kind. Further and further from the portal he flew. Still nothing. No sight of any type of a dwelling. No other natives. Just mountains and valleys and trees as far as the eye could see.

A dark blotch on the ground caught his keen eye.

A shelter?

The sun was beginning to set. The cold was getting colder, and the woman in his claws was feeling the bite of the wind much worse than him. Even holding her close to his warm chest wasn't enough. His innate dragon senses could tell her core temperature was dropping rapidly. Unless he wanted to kill her himself, he needed to find shelter and warm her up quickly.

Protect, his dragon snarled, curling his claws tighter around the precious cargo clutched to his chest.

Col circled back to the dark square he'd seen a few minutes ago. He landed nearby in a clearing a short distance away in the safety of the trees. No need to make himself known without checking the perimeter first.

Tucking his wings tight to his back, he moved through the forest, careful to keep his large body and tail from destroying his surroundings and giving away his position. He tucked his mate safely against his chest with one claw and moved forward carefully on three legs. Having her with him was slowing him down, but he couldn't bring himself to leave her alone while he scouted the shelter.

He crept closer, until he'd reached the clearing in front of the shelter. It wasn't huge, but it was definitely better than trying to camp in the open. The roof was almost completely covered by the white powder. There were drifts that covered halfway up the outside walls, but he could still see the door. It wouldn't take much for his dragon to dig a way in. No fresh scents were in the area. The trace odors of the natives who'd built it were months old. No one was living here now.

Col relaxed just a little and walked further into the clearing toward the shelter. It appeared to be made from logs. There was a single window on the front, made of clear glass. A stack of firewood was buried under the cold white powder on one side. He put the woman down close to the stacked wood, where he'd be able to see her as he dug out the front door. Then used his large claws to move the powder away from the doorway of the shelter.

"W-what the—"

He swung his big head toward the sound.

His mate had come to and was staring at him with big wide brown eyes full of fear.

"Oh my God!" Her voice trembled and shook, fluttering like the smallest of butterflies.

He liked the rich tone of her voice. Even frightened, it

soothed his angry mind. For a moment, all that existed was her. Everything else faded into the background.

Col put his big nose closer to her body but froze when she covered her mouth to muffle a scream. He didn't want to hurt her or frighten her further, but his dragon liked her. Wanted to breathe in her scent. Taste her.

"Please don't eat me." She pressed herself backward into the woodpile, as if willing her body to become one with the logs.

The words started to coalesce. His Reylean magick was working hard, putting together a giant puzzle in his mind. She hadn't spoken enough yet. He needed her to speak more words to help him solidify the language in his mind.

Her teeth were chattering now. Whether from fear or the cold, it didn't matter; he needed to get her inside. Get a fire started. Get her warmed.

He turned back to the door and finished digging away all the cold, wet, white powder. It melted on contact with his warm skin. Once clear, he shifted to his two-legged form and went back to the woman.

"You're a person? How can you be a dragon *and* a person?" She was hugging herself. Her curls stuck out from all angles around the bandage he'd wrapped her head with. Her face was flush with color and her eyes were wide, like that of a deer before being caught. "Please don't hurt me."

"I have no intention of hurting you," he spoke slowly, trying out the new tongue. It was choppy and flowed strangely from his lips. "The others I hunt. They attacked you."

"Wait... So, there's more than one of you here? More dragons?"

Hadn't she seen Jaha and his sister? They'd injured her. Why was she acting as though he was the first dragon she'd seen?

"I hunt two traitors of the house of Li'Vhram. I'd still be hunting them, but they injured you." He approached slowly. "You need warmth, *shuarra*. Let me help you inside."

She flinched and shook her head.

"I will not injure you." His voice was harder that time, laced with impatience. She might still be afraid of him, but he wasn't going to stand here in the cold arguing and trying to coax her into trusting him. He bent down, scooped up her flailing body and crossed to the door.

"Hey! Help!" Her cry pierced not only his ear, but his heart as well.

He was trying to help her. He would never hurt a woman ... well, except Jaha's sister. Col intended to hurt Sefa. But her death would be quick, unlike the plans he had to pull Jaha apart one limb at a time.

"I *am* helping you." He kept his voice level. She was like a wounded animal, unpredictable and dangerous to herself. "You are injured. Stop struggling." She needed to calm. Fighting him was only going to make her more stressed and her head injury bleed more. Her heart was racing again, and he could smell the fresh blood seeping from her wound. "Stop." he said again, meeting her frightened gaze with the same fierce one he used on the warriors in training beneath him in his father's guard.

She stilled in his arms, and the cries turned into muffled whimpers.

Better.

Yanking hard, he pulled out the padlock from the door and moved inside the shelter. Light filtered in from several windows. The walls and ceiling were all bare wood but sealed against the wind. There was a bed in the back and another door. A couch sat directly to his left and to his right was a stone fireplace, which pleased him.

He needed to get a fire started immediately.

Further back to the right was a small table and a few cabinets. Perhaps they'd hold basic supplies, if not; he'd hunt and feed his *shuarra*. Once she was taken care of, he'd resume the hunt for the traitors. They wouldn't be far. They wanted him dead as much as he desired to end them.

"Where are we? Do you live out here?" she asked, her voice quieter and more controlled this time. "Who are you?"

"I don't know where we are." Col looked down at her in confusion. "Why don't you know?" This was her world. She should have a general idea of where she was. "Where is the closest town?"

She shook her head. "My head hurts so bad." Tears welled in her eyes again. "I can't even remember my name. Everything just hurts."

"Just rest. It will come back to you." He laid her on the bed and pulled the extra blanket up to cover her. "I will get wood for the fire and warm this place up. Are you going to run?"

"Out into the freezing snow? In the middle of

nowhere, when I don't know where I am or who I am?" She gave him a brave half-chuckle, and he felt his heart give a small leap of hope that she would not remain terrified of him. "I may have amnesia, but I'm not stupid. As long as you promise you're not here to eat me."

"I do not eat people." Even though Reyleans often fought in animal form, enemies were never consumed *on purpose.* In the heat of the battle anything could happen, especially with dragons. Most of the other animals weren't big enough to just swallow a person.

"Good to know."

"Snow? Is that the name you call the white powder?" He changed the subject and focused on the unknown word she'd used to describe the landscape. Most of the language was obvious, but there were elements about the world he wouldn't understand without an explanation.

She cocked her head and stared at him from beneath the blanket. "You don't know what snow is?"

"There is none on my world."

"It's frozen water. Falls in the winter like rain." She took a deep breath, calming her racing heartbeat further. He was impressed at her self-control. "I don't think dragons are real. I'm probably just hallucinating you and this cabin and...everything."

"You are safe with me. I will not let the traitors near you again." He backed up a few steps. "I will return."

"Wait." Her voice teetered on breaking, like a large tree limb under the force of a thousand pounds just before it snapped. "Who are you?"

"I am Col of the House of Li'Vhram."

"And the other people ... the dragons you're chasing... They hurt me? Hurt your family?"

He nodded, impressed that even with a head injury she was attempting to put things together around her. She was strong.

Mine. Claim.

Col mentally shoved his dragon's voice down and held back his snarl of anger. His dragon would obey. This woman might be Fate's choice for him as a mate, but there was no time for claiming.

He'd made his vow. Justice would be served for his family, and only the blood of Jaha and Sefa would satisfy that vow. "I must get wood for the fire. Stay still."

He turned on his heel and slipped out the front door before she could ask another question, or his dragon pushed more. Being in the woman's presence was difficult. Her soul called to him, and the more he looked at her, the worse it became. The harder it got to push down his dragon.

Everything inside him wanted to touch her. Hold her again. He wanted to bury his face in her hair and fill his lungs with her scent so that he would never forget it.

No.

He stalked down the front of the shelter, his boots crunching in the thick inches of snow. The woodpile was covered in it. All the logs were wet from the *snow*. Frozen water.

Col quickly made a small stack of firewood a short distance from the house, shifted to his dragon form and breathed a quick flash fire over the logs. The snow on the ground around the small stack melted instantly. Steam hissed, and the logs crackled, but within a minute they were dry, and the outsides turned black as ash. They would burn well now.

He shifted back to his human form, scooped up the logs, slightly charred and still red hot in places. The fire didn't bother him though. His skin was impervious to flame or heat of any kind. A nice addition to the strength of his tribe that kept dragons from turning their fire on each other in a fight. Completely useless. It wouldn't even burn off clothes. Their magick protected any covering they were wearing like armor.

He opened the door to the cabin. The bed was empty. The woman was gone.

Col threw the logs at the hearth, and then crossed the cabin to the bed. Her scent was strong and led... He turned to the door in the back. His shoulders sagged with unwanted relief. She was behind the door. He could hear her moving around, then the sound of running water.

He opened the door and peered inside.

She stood with her back to him at a white stone bowl that had water running from a silver mouth.

Fascinated, he stepped inside the small room. To his left was a glass box in the corner.

She met his gaze in the mirror hanging on the wall over the water bowl.

His mate had a cloth in her hand and was dabbing at the wound on the back of her neck.

Help.

He agreed. She shouldn't have to clean herself up when he was here to take care of her.

"Let me." He took the wet cloth from her hand before

she could object. Col ran it under the ice-cold water coming from the silver mouth, and then pushed aside a few of her silky brown curls so he could see the cut on the back of her head.

It wasn't deep, but whatever her head had struck nicked a blood vessel. Head wounds were always messy.

His mouth went dry. His cock went hard. His every sense tuned to her.

Her hair was so soft on his fingers. Her scent filled his lungs. He fought himself to keep from leaning down and rubbing his cheek against her curls. She was injured. She wasn't even herself. She didn't remember her name or anything about why she was out in the wilderness by herself.

"Thanks." The word was hesitant, but not fearful.

Col nodded and wiped at the crusted blood, cleaning it from her hair and neck. The wound looked good. The bleeding had stopped and was closing up nicely already. "It was not deep, but it was enough to damage your memory. You hit something very hard."

She chuckled a little. "Nothing like waking up in the wilderness with nothing but a sexy, wild dragon man who insists on taking care of you. I feel like I'm in some sort of fantasy flick."

"A flick?"

"A movie. A story with pictures that you watch on a screen."

He nodded but wondered why they would *watch* stories instead of just telling them at gatherings.

The other word—sexy—he didn't have a meaning for that either. It sounded like a positive description. Her tone had been positive. Just the fact that she was letting him touch her without completely losing her mind was progress in and of itself. No screaming or weeping. He'd take it.

"You are clean." He reluctantly set the cloth down on the side of the bowl. The last thing he wanted to do was *quit* touching her.

She took it, rinsed it and then hung it again on the side. Then turned to him and stared, like she was waiting for him to do something.

Col stepped closer. His hands went into her hair, stroking through the silky curls. He rubbed a thumb over the angular line of her cheek. Her skin was so soft. He just couldn't stop himself.

She stood frozen in place. Her eyes widened, but she didn't object. Didn't run. Didn't scream and yell and tell him to stop. She should've.

It would've been easier to tell his dragon no if she fought him. Instead, after a moment she leaned her head into the palm of his hand.

"Thank you for not leaving me out there alone. I know I kinda went off on you and freaked out. I'm still not sure that I'm not hallucinating the whole thing. Maybe I'm still lying out there somewhere in the snow, unconscious, and you're just my dying fantasy."

Her voice was low and husky with unrealized desire, but Col could hear it. His dragon could hear it. Magick surged between them, and the glow of her soul called to his so strongly, for a moment. he could think of nothing else.

"The way you look at me is like a fantasy. So intense

and hungry. It's like the second you saw me, you fell in love with me. Which is crazy. Also, why I think you're just a fantasy in my mind. Plus, dragons aren't real. And, I have no memory of who I am."

"You are not dying. Dragons are real in my world. And I do want you, but you are ill and need to rest." Col dropped his hand away from her face but froze when she put a palm flat on his chest.

She anchored him in place.

His feet wouldn't respond to the commands his brain was giving. *Get away. Stop her.*

Mine. Mate. His dragon insisted. *Claim.*

"What if I said I wanted you?" Her tone was soft but daring. Her fingers trailed down his bare chest, leaving burning trails of desire in their wake.

His entire body came to life. His skin rippled as his dragon tried to press to the surface.

Col breathed deeply and caught his mate by the wrist. "You don't know what you're asking for, *shuarra*." His dragon purred within his chest, pleased that the man had let himself call her his *mate* again. Col, was less so. He couldn't have her yet, not until he'd carried out justice for his family. "You are injured. You should rest." He made a slight move backward, but she stepped closer, pressing her body against his.

He still held her wrist out to the side of their bodies, but now he could feel *all* of her against him. Even through the puffy covering shielding her upper body, he could feel the softness of her breasts. Her hips hit just below his and her belly pressed in agonizingly against his hard cock.

"What's that word mean? *Shuarra*?" She lifted her chin. Her hungry gaze met his without abandon.

The *soul call* between them was so strong. Stronger than he'd realized at first.

"Mate." His tone was heavy with desire for the woman in front of him.

His justice would have to wait.

CHAPTER
THREE

COL

Col slipped his arms around his mate's body and pulled her closer, away from the white wash bowl. He slanted his mouth over hers and claimed it, thrusting his tongue deep and tasting her sweet flavor. The kiss wasn't rough and angry, more like demanding. He was staking a claim.

She was his. Would be his.

He imagined how it would be to kiss his mate like this every day for the rest of his life. His hands moved to her hips, pulling her closer, pushing his body into hers. She was so soft. So welcoming.

He released her hips for a second, but only long enough to work the fastenings on her covering. Col opened it and pushed it down from her shoulders until it fell to the hard, bare floor. Then he pulled her against him again, her breasts soft and firm against his chest beneath her remaining clothing. So perfect. Only, he wanted to see more of her skin. More of the glow that called to his soul. Wanted to kiss and taste her entire body.

There was no hesitation in her kiss. Her mouth moved against his, tangling and tasting his mouth as he had with hers.

Col nipped at her lips, then moved to the soft exposed skin of her neck. Not now, but soon he would mark her as his own. No other male would come near her if she bore his bite mark—his scent would forever be mixed with hers.

Yes. His dragon agreed.

She moaned into his mouth and blood rushed to his cock. No way had she missed the way his hard erection was pressed into the soft roundness of her belly. The sounds she made. The soft mewls and cries as he nipped and kissed his way down her neck to where her shirt began.

Thoughts of ripping it off crossed his mind, but instead he grabbed the bottom and tugged it up and off. She'd need her clothes when they left this shelter.

His *shuarra* gasped and shivered. The cold air made her beautiful sandy colored skin tighten. Bumps rose along her arms and torso, and around the strange bit of fabric that she wore to encase her breasts.

Col looked for a tie to remove the thin covering. "Off." He growled deep in his chest, pulling at one of the shoulder straps. It didn't come loose, and he couldn't see how to remove it.

Her arms folded behind her back and a second later the fabric came loose.

He pulled it down her arms, freeing her beautiful, full breasts. Her nipples were pink and erect and begging for his mouth. His stomach tightened, like someone had landed a well-aimed fist to his mid-section. She was a gift from Fate. More than he could have ever imagined. Energy surged through his veins, a rush not unlike what he felt during battle. Or while he was soaring through the skies of Reylea.

This woman was his new home.

She put her hands into his long hair as he licked and sucked and worshiped her breasts. The little gasps and moans drove him further.

The way her fingertips traced over his face and ear and neck. She drew circles on his arm, following the lines of his family markings. Ink he'd earned as he'd advanced through the levels of his warrior training.

The way she touched him ... so soft, but inquisitive. Curious. It drove the lust inside him even higher. His heart hammered in his chest. His cock throbbed with the overwhelming need to sink deep into his *shuarra*. To claim her as his own. He'd never known such desire.

Not in all his years. Not with any woman.

His mate was different. Her soul was his alone. Fate had chosen her to glow just for him. It was a gift and a promise he could no longer ignore. Perhaps it was Fate's way of telling him he shouldn't desire vengeance. His vow still stood. He *would* seek his family's justice, but he'd keep his mate safe and close as well.

The light emanating from her tan skin illuminated the shadows of this small washroom, but only for him. She couldn't see it. Probably for the best too.

The window behind her was the only other source of light and it was quickly fading. The sun had already fallen behind the distant peaks.

Col growled, wrapping his hands around her body, lifting her from the floor. There was a bed in the other room. He wanted a chance to fully enjoy his mate.

He took three steps and laid her out on the bed. Her legs had wrapped around his hips, and he took pleasure in rocking toward her as if he were already sinking his cock deep into her heat.

She whimpered and cried and begged softly for more, saying his name over and over again like it was the only word she knew.

Col leaned down to kiss her bare stomach, and then trailed kisses up her ribcage, to where her breasts waited for more attention. Her pink nipples were hard. He cupped both in his hands, loving the way they fit perfectly in his palms. He thumbed over her nipples.

She gasped for breath. "Col." Her voice shimmered, beautiful and erotic and heavy with desire.

"*Shuarra*," he said, using the only name he had for her. The only one that truly mattered. She was *his*. He dipped down and took one of her nipples into his mouth again, caressing and nibbling just hard enough to make her gasp over and over and over.

She writhed beneath him, rising up to capture his head in her hands as a long moan of pleasure tore through her chest. A sheen of sweat had broken out across her brow, cheeks, and torso. The slight salty taste only added to her perfect flavor on his tongue.

He sampled her other breast and she cried out again.

"Please." Desperation grew in her voice, rocketing his pulse. She was not Reylean. She didn't know about the way souls glowed and called to their mates in his world. But he could tell she felt the need as strongly as he did. Felt the way the magick pulled them together.

He put his mouth on one breast, cupping it with one hand, while his other went to the fastener at the front on her leg coverings. It came undone without much trouble and he worked at the metal teeth below the fastener until they came apart as well.

Then he slid his hand beneath her bottom, grabbed the top of her coverings and pulled them down with one effortless stroke. Something remained; something bright pink covered her pussy. Col grabbed that too and yanked it down, tossing it to the floor with the rest.

Now she was glorious and bared to him completely. He parted her legs and brushed his lips reverently across the lips of her sex. A smattering of brown curls teased him.

She stilled on the bed, panting for breath. She smelled amazing. Clean and sweet and perfectly woman.

His woman. His *shuarra*.

He parted her damp folds and licked, drawing his tongue slowly over her swollen clit. Even though she wasn't Reylean, she was similar in every way to their females' forms.

She gasped and whimpered and writhed beneath his mouth.

Col continued to lash her with his tongue, holding her in place, taking his pleasure by giving pleasure to her.

"Col, please." Her body trembled beneath the powerful hold of his arms.

He kept one arm across her hips, stopping her from wriggling away. With the other hand, he slid two fingers inside her slick wet warmth, exploring. In and out. Slowly then faster, mimicking how he'd fill her with his cock very soon. "You are beautiful, my *shuarra*. Fly for me." His voice rolled from his chest, dark and commanding.

Col curled his fingers inside her, loving the feel of each shudder and clench of her thighs. He flicked his tongue over her clit again, moving his free hand to the other breast where he pinched and rolled her nipples just enough to make her moan.

Her body tightened again. The orgasm was rising, pulling her to the very top. She panted and gasped, "Col. Col, I need—" She dropped her head as another cry ripped from her throat.

He stilled his fingers as her body tightened around them. Then took her clit into his mouth and gave her what she needed.

She bucked off the bed beneath his hold as she came. The keening cry made him feel more alive than he'd ever felt before.

His name on her lips was the most powerful magick he'd ever experienced. He wouldn't leave her. Ever. He'd stay with his *shuarra* until the day he died.

"Ohmygod." She shuddered violently and fell back on the mattress with a satisfied sigh.

Col released her hip and crawled up over her body, lifting her small form and dragging her up toward the head of the bed. Then he kissed her again, taking her mouth. Slowly. Deeply. Enjoying each mewl and cry that squeaked out of her.

Her hands went to the waist of his kilt, fumbling and exploring, looking for a way to unfasten it.

"If I'm naked, you need to be," she whispered on a breath against his lips.

He reached for the knot at his hip and worked it loose without releasing her mouth. He didn't want to miss a single moment of tasting her.

The leather and fabric kilt came loose and fell from his hips, leaving nothing for her imagination to consider. His cock was long and hard, and he wanted nothing more than to drive it deep into her right in that moment. His tip dragged along the velvety smooth skin of her hip.

Her fingers dug into the meat of his arms, and she arched off the bed, thrusting her hips closer. "Col, please. I need you inside me so badly it hurts."

Col nudged her opening with his cock, pressing forward just a little to make sure she could take him. A little more. Then a little more.

Her body stilled as she stretched to accommodate his girth. She was tight and needy. The fire in her eyes locked with his as he pushed further. Her mouth opened in a wide "O" that turned to a moan. Her figure quivered next, anticipation building from within.

Her eyes were wide as he sank deeper, slowly, inch by inch until he was seated all the way to the base. She fit him like a glove. Her skin glowed and glistened.

She was the most beautiful woman he'd ever seen. She was his.

His hips rolled into hers and she groaned, digging her

fingernails into his biceps. He slid out, nearly all the way, before pushing in again.

It was like he'd found what had been missing his whole life.

"Watch me," he ordered. "See me claim you, *shuarra*."

Her big brown eyes locked with his gaze as he drove into her harder than before.

Col relished the way her hands clawed at his arms, his shoulders, anything she could reach from where he'd pinned her to the bed. The slight pain of her fingernails only increased his desire.

He pushed her legs, guiding them around his waist.

She wrapped them tightly, lifting her hips off the bed.

He wrapped an arm around her shoulders and lifted the rest of her until she was straddling his thighs as she rode him.

Her arms were around his neck and his face was buried between her gorgeous breasts. He licked and sucked and bit at her nipples until she rocked up and down. Then he took hold of her hips and slammed her down hard.

She cried out as he lifted her again and then pulled her right back down. "Col!" Her body was tightening, winding its way closer and closer to release.

He wasn't going to last much longer, but he wanted her to come first. Wanted to feel her bear down as she found her climax. "Fly for me again, *shuarra*. Now." He growled deep in his chest and bit down a little harder on one of her nipples. The pain was just enough to push her over the edge.

She screamed, digging her fingers into his back, then

screamed again, wave after wave of her climax rolling through her to him.

He laid her back on the bed, driving into her again and again as she came, his mouth moving closer and closer to the soft curve where her neck met her shoulder.

She came again with another furious cry of need and pleasure all wrapped into one.

Col joined her this time, a roar tearing from his throat. His balls tightened and then heat poured through his body until it erupted, filling her with his seed, marking her as his mate.

His dragon fangs lengthened, and he bit down on her shoulder, tasting her blood, sealing her to him.

Forever.

It could never be undone.

FOUR

NAOMI

Her eyes opened slowly. Wooden walls. Wooden ceiling. *Cabin.* Fabric beneath her body. A mattress. She was in a bed. Her skin was clammy and warm. She was soaked with sweat. Gentle pressure on her lips—ceramic—made her open her mouth. Cold water dribbled through them. She swallowed.

Then everything came rushing back.

Great beasts—a red and a black dragon—had fallen from the sky right into the clearing where she was trying to photograph Alaskan wildlife.

Pretty sure dragons were not native to the valley. They'd seen her. Chased her into the trees. She'd thought for sure she was about to be a reptilian snack. Then everything had just gone black.

The next thing she remembered was another dragon

setting her gently down in front of an old snow-covered cabin. He was black also, but much bigger than the first one that'd attacked her with the red. Then he'd been a man. How was that possible?

Of course, that was saying that dragons were possible too. She wasn't ready to admit to the existence of either.

"*Shuarra*?" The rumbly dark sexy voice from her dreams was speaking to her again.

He'd made her feel safe. Desired. She'd dream-walked through the best sex of her life. Whatever had happened to her head, she wanted it again.

The air held the scent of sweat and...

Emotions slammed into her head, drowning her in pain and guilt. How could sex with a stranger have been better than what she'd had with the love of her life?

But it *had* been.

She'd loved Tommy since grade school. They'd been planning a wedding. A family.

Everything.

Then the accident had taken him from her. Had taken *everything* from her. She never thought she'd have another chance at being happy. At feeling anything close to what she'd felt with Tommy. She didn't want to. She didn't deserve to.

It'd been her fault Tommy had been in the car when he was.

She had sent him to his death...

"Ohmygod!" Naomi sat up straight. She was in a bed. Her lungs clamped down, like a vise was tightening on them. It couldn't be real. But *he* was right there. The man from her dreams, the *dragon* who'd saved her was sitting on the edge of the bed with a cup in his hand.

Everything came tumbling back.

He'd said he was hunting the first two dragons. That he wasn't from this world. That kiss in the bathroom. Then sex ... mind-blowing, earth-shattering, crazy hot sex with a dragon man. And—he'd made her forget. Well, she'd had amnesia. For a few moments she'd felt what it was like to be held and loved by a man.

It'd been so long.

A dull throbbing pain between her neck and her shoulder brought her out of her memories. She turned to the man at the foot of the bed. "You bit me!" She craned her neck trying to get a look at the shoulder he'd sunk his teeth into. She remembered feeling the pain through the fog of her incredible orgasm, but nothing after that. Her body had been so heavy and tired. Sleep had been the only option.

She traced her fingers along her bare left shoulder. There were four puncture marks, two on the front and two on the back. She could feel the ridges where a scar had formed. "How long was I out?" she asked.

The beautiful man with bronze skin and black tattoos swirling up and down his arms, cocked his head and paused a moment before answering.

His name was Col. She recalled from her muddled memories.

"You have been asleep several hours. My bite seems to have caused a fever in your body."

She nodded. "Everything burns. Why would you bite me?" Naomi pulled the blanket up to cover her breasts.

"And how are the holes from your teeth already healed?"

"You're mine, *shuarra*." He yanked the blanket down and leaned into her personal space. "My mate. Do not hide yourself. You are beautiful and have the most exquisite breasts." Col dipped his head. His mouth closed around one of her nipples and he suckled on her, sending sparks straight south.

Her mouth opened, and she panted. Naomi's core ached and throbbed from the sex they'd had hours before. Now, she'd be damned if her body wasn't craving more like an addict that desperately needed their next hit.

"No, no, no," she protested, shoving his head away, but missing the warmth of his mouth on her the moment it came off her breast.

How could she want this? Another man.

Tommy had been her whole world. No one could replace him. Ever. But all she could think about was *this* man's presence. How big and strong and muscled and exciting.

It was the first time since Tommy's death two years ago that she'd actually felt alive. Her family had begged her to get away. Take some time for herself.

She'd avoided everyone and everything, except her job. This Alaska shoot had come up at the magazine where she worked. It'd originally been given to an intern, but for some reason she'd begged her editor for the opportunity.

Something deep inside her had needed to get away. From the city. From her grief. From her inability to move forward in life without Tommy. And now that it'd worked ... now that she had taken that first step, she felt like a traitor. A rock sat in the bottom of her stomach, weighing her down, pulling her even further away from the present.

"What saddens you?"

"I—" Naomi started, then stared at the man sitting a foot away from her. Was she that obvious? She'd learned to bury her emotions and hide them from her family. At least that was what she told herself.

Mostly, they just accused her of avoiding them. Even her friends at work accused her of becoming a shut-in. So, what if she had? She didn't deserve to be happy. She'd killed her fiancé. He'd died, and she'd just been left alone and lost.

A low rumble made her look back at Col again, but she didn't want to talk about Tommy.

"You can't distract me away from the fact that you bit me. You might be sexy and covered in muscles and have a really magnificent cock, but I'm going to need more explanations now that I'm ... me."

He sat back, giving her space immediately. "You remember?"

"Yep, dragons falling from the sky. Check. Getting ass kicked by aforementioned dragons. Check. You bringing me here to this abandoned cabin and telling me you were hunting the dragons that attacked me. Please feel free to butt in at any time and tell me I'm just on some drug, tripping so high, I don't know up from down. Then we had mind-altering sex. And I woke up, right now, with all my memories intact."

"I don't understand all the words you said, *shuarra*, but you seem to have the order of events correct in your mind."

His voice was like a purr, and she wanted to rub all over him like a cat in heat.

"What the heck is wrong with me?" Why couldn't she control her desire? Why couldn't she just shut down this feeling burning inside her?

She'd had sex for the first time in two years because she'd had amnesia. Well, that was over. Now she should be able to get back to work. Focus on her career. Nothing more. She didn't need anything more.

Liar. The little voice in the back of her mind spat out. *Fine.* Maybe she was lying to herself. It didn't remove the feeling she'd betrayed Tommy—was *still* betraying Tommy—by letting this stranger touch her, pleasure her, make her forget...

A hint of a satisfied smile curved the corner of Col's mouth.

Naomi narrowed her gaze and gave him her best tell-me-now-or-else look. It didn't affect him in the least.

"You are my mate. Your soul glowed for mine. We are sealed together forever. I will protect you with my life until the day I die."

Mate?

Hold the freaking horses. She did *not* agree with that.

And well, fuck.

She wanted to yell and rant and tell him he'd had no right to make that choice for her. Except she remembered very clearly *telling* him she wanted it. Wanted him.

But I didn't want a mate. I had my chance and lost it.

The biting and claiming were a bit overboard. Couldn't they have just had monumental sex and called it an amazing fling?

Naomi hadn't been looking for one. But now... Now she was shacked up in the middle of nowhere, naked and horny for the dragon man sitting at the foot of the bed, smiling at her like he knew her thoughts had drifted into the gutter. Again.

At least he wasn't naked. That one small detail was helping her control her carnal urges just a tiny bit.

He'd put his barbarian kilt thing on again. He was probably cold. Even with the fire burning across the room, the air still had a very icy chill to it. Typical January in inland Alaska—or so she'd read.

Not that the chill was cooling off her horniness in the least. Her nipples were puckered and needy beneath the blanket. Her arousal was slicking her thighs. She needed some damn clothes. Staying on the bed naked was only going to keep her mind on the super-hot, half-naked, dragon-man in the room.

"Look, I'm going to need my clothes back. And then a ride back to where I had my shoot set up. I have a snowmachine back there. And hopefully my camera is still intact. I'll be out of your hair and back to town in a jiffy. Then you can get back to your *hunting*, right? Win, win."

"Your shoot?"

"I'm a photographer. I was out here on assignment for a nature magazine."

Col shook his head, obviously not understanding.

"I take pictures. Art."

"An artist," he repeated. "What was left behind in the snow? I didn't see anything."

"My stuff is back there. It's expensive. So, let's just call this a wrap." Naomi grabbed her panties off the floor.

Where the hell are the rest of my clothes?

She slipped on the panties, trying to keep the rest of herself modestly hidden. It didn't work. With only one arm to cover both boobs and a pair of panties that refused to slide up her legs, she flashed him everything more than once.

"You are my mate, *shuarra*." He stepped forward, taking the hem of her panties and pulling them up into place.

His warm fingers lingered on her skin, and she wished for a moment that more of his thermal skin was touching her. Wished his whole body was wrapped around her, warming her all the way through to her soul. Excitement rippled through her heart, tingling along the surface of her skin, as if she were awakening for the very first time. Just for this man—dragon—just for Col.

"My name is Naomi, by the way. Naomi Parker. Not that I don't like the *shuarra* name, especially the way you sorta purr it out like a big cat. Ohmygod. I'm doing it again. It's like I'm sixteen and can't control my hormones. I'm pretty sure if you keep touching me right now, I'm going to completely lose it. Can you hand me my pants, please?" She pointed to the corner of the floor where they'd been tossed during their dynamic lovemaking session. Maybe he would just ignore all of the word-vomit pouring from her mouth.

Mouth. His mouth. His tongue.

Damn. Her mind was in the gutter again.

The man knew how to use his mouth. And his fingers. And his ... cock. Okay, everything. Col knew how to use everything and everything on her body felt used. There were little red marks all over her breasts and her hips from his teeth.

Her pussy was sore and well-used. It had been. She remembered every exhilarating moment of ecstasy.

And, her unused-underappreciated-girly-bits were hungry for more.

"These?" He picked up the pants from the corner.

"Yes, pants."

He returned and knelt, allowing her to slip one foot in at a time. Then she stood, still holding the blanket against her chest to cover her boobs.

He pulled up the ice-cold denim jeans and she tried to hold back a gasp, but the chill from the half-frozen fabric temporarily sucked all the warmth from her entire body like a dip into an ice bath. Chill bumps sprouted all over her body.

"Naomi is a beautiful name, my *shuarra.*"

"Thank you. But, back to what I was asking. You'll take me back to where you found me?" she asked, hoping to capitalize on his positive mood. "And I still need my bra and my sweater and coat."

He shook his head. "You are safer hidden here. I must fight the traitors before they injure anyone else in your world. They are dangerous. And my responsibility." Col grabbed her hand and tugged. "Come sit and warm yourself by the fire." He paused, his gaze dropping to her chest. "Unless you would like me to crawl back into bed with you and warm you a different way."

"Ho, buddy, eyes up here. I may have a boob hanging out, but I need your attention." Naomi could've sworn he smirked before meeting her gaze and nearly boring a hole through her with the intensity of his stare. Brown eyes flecked with metallic gold. So beautiful. So un-earthly.

She shook her head, trying to put her thoughts back in order.

Stop thinking about the gorgeous dragon man.

"I just need to get back to my stuff and back down the mountain. I'll come back out later and get the pictures I need."

Hopefully, all the dragons will be gone in a few days.

Though after saying it like that, it sounded ridiculous. They'd just arrived. Why would they leave? And how many were there really? Just three?

Col and these other two traitors as he called them. That seemed unlikely.

Also, dragons were real. That was still not truly computing in the brain.

"It is not safe." His voice was more of a growl again. He stood and paced to the end of the cabin room and then back to the foot of the bed. "If you go outside, they will pick up your scent."

"There's nothing here. No food. No way to contact anyone. I'll freeze."

He snarled, obviously not liking her protests.

Naomi pondered a moment and changed tactics. "What if something happens to you? I'll die up here. No one will ever find me. And I'll never get down off this mountain alone without equipment."

"You are not alone. I am here."

"But you keep saying you're leaving to hunt those other dragons. What about me?"

"This cabin is safe."

"No," she insisted. "This is someone's cabin. We're lucky there's even water. Most of these cabins are dry. This one has a tankless water heater and an indoor tank. Somebody spent some money on this place. Which means they probably won't leave it empty for long. So, I guess if you want strangers to take care of me."

What the ... what am I saying? And when did the dragon man become *not* a stranger? *After the wild sex?*

Was she really entertaining the idea that she might want a man again? That she wanted Col to take care of her? That she didn't want to go back to the monotonous sadness that had enveloped her life since Tommy's death? Or allow the lung-crushing, paralyzing weight that'd threatened to suffocate her for the last two years to return.

Could she really move forward ... with a dragon?

How did she not think she was crazy? If she wasn't crazy, and Col was real and not a fantasy in her mind, did she really think there was an option to stay with the barbarian dragon guy? What was he going to do for a job?

She sighed. Staying with him wasn't realistic.

Was it? Her mother's voice echoed in her mind. *Would Tommy want you to live your life unhappy? What would he say if he saw you today?*

Naomi shoved down the thoughts. She couldn't love

anyone but Tommy. It wasn't possible, and she didn't deserve the chance. Staying with a dragon man from another world was on a whole different level than trying to get out there and date again. It was crazy. *She* was being crazy.

"Look, you have your business to take care of, and I can't stay here. So, take me back to my stuff or I'm walking out on my own."

"Not yet." Col's eyes flashed solid gold and he snarled. Not at her, just in general. He stalked over to her, picked her up, and carried her back to the bed. He laid her down and pressed his body over hers.

His mouth crushed hers, and his taste flooded her senses. She was locked between his powerful arms. One hand cupped her face, directing the kiss. His other hand had ripped away the blanket and was now kneading her breast, squeezing and flicking at her traitorously hard nipple. A whimper escaped into his mouth. He tasted so good.

What'd she been complaining about? Being crazy?

Maybe a little crazy was just what she needed. Maybe this was Fate's way of giving her a kick in the ass.

The only thing Naomi could concentrate on right now was the length of Col's hard cock pressing into her belly, and the way his tongue plunged in and out of her mouth like a promise of what was to come.

His kiss was intoxicating. His hands felt cool against her burning skin. The need for him was primal. Desperate. She wanted to feel alive. Somehow, he was giving her that. For now, she'd take it.

"Col."

His mouth trailed from her lips to her ear and down her neck. Every touch was tender and demanding at the same time. He was trying to shut down her argument with him about leaving the cabin. And—surprise—she was totally fine with allowing it.

"I need—" Her voice carried a deeper and huskier quality than she'd ever heard before. What did she need? What did she want from Col? More distraction?

It felt like *more* than that.

He reared his head up and smiled down, then crawled down the length of her body. Her pants and panties were quickly stripped off again.

So much for getting dressed.

Then his mouth was between her legs again.

Naomi cried out and bucked her hips, but he held her in place, erotically torturing her pussy until her whole body shook with more need.

His fingers slipped inside and stroked, finding just the right angle.

She pushed her head back into the pillows and moaned as his mouth closed around her clit. "Ohhhhhh—"

His tongue flicked deftly across her, driving her higher and higher.

Bliss was so close. She could feel it wrapping its warm tendrils of pleasure around her whole body.

Everything slowed. Every stroke of his fingers and tongue left her breathless, but desperate for more.

"Yes," she panted. "Yes," she screamed, bucking against his hold.

Heat and tension blasted through her like a race car

jumping from zero to sixty. Stars exploded behind her eyes. Pleasure washed over her in waves.

Col kept sucking and licking and stroking. It was so much.

She screamed again as he wrung yet another climax from her body.

"Mine. You will not leave me." He crawled up her body and stared. Waiting.

Naomi nodded. She wanted this with every fiber of her being. *All* of it. Whatever came with it. She couldn't go back to being an empty sad shell. Even if this wasn't permanent, she wanted to experience everything she could with Col. She wanted to feel alive again.

"Vow it." His eyes flickering gold. The dragon was impatient for an answer.

"I won't leave you." It was a promise. Every tone. Every syllable. She didn't want to be alone for the rest of her life. Haunted by the memory of the man and love she'd lost.

Tommy wouldn't have wanted that for her either. It was killing her family too. Every time they looked at her, the pity cut to the bone.

Not anymore. Whatever her dragon man wanted. That was fine by her. If Col was the trade-off, she could manage the guilt.

You're lying to yourself.

No, she wasn't. She could be happy. She could. She would. Naomi had never cared enough to try.

Col made her want to try.

The choice lifted a weight from her chest. "I need you, Col."

He huffed out a loud breath and flipped her to her stomach.

She turned and watched him over her shoulder, quivering in anticipation.

His hands trailed over her back, then to her ass, kneading and pinching as they went. He was so beautiful. The swirling tattoos. The rippling muscles. How the hell had she ended up right where he would be in the middle of Alaska?

Her mind drifted back to the way he was caressing her ass. He gripped her hips, lifting her up toward him. She watched as he removed the kilt. His massive cock sprang forward and bumped against her aching clit. She wiggled her hips, rubbing against it.

Col grasped the erection and guided it to her opening. Slowly. Gently. He pressed forward, filling her inch by solid inch until his hips were flush to her ass. Then he pulled backward with excruciating slowness.

"Col," she panted, "Please."

His hands clenched down on her hips and then he drove deep and hard. Naomi bowed under him, and he bent down over her back, thrusting and driving until she could feel nothing but him. Inside her. Around her. His hands clutched her so tightly to his body that it felt as though they were one being.

One of his hands slid around her hip and brushed between her thighs. One little touch. That was all it took to send her careening over the cliff.

She screamed his name and he roared hers, an animalistic carnal sound that shook her to the core, but instead of making her afraid, she just felt even safer.

More content. More satisfied.

They slumped together, Col's cock still inside her as he rolled to the side pulling her with him.

She fit perfectly against him. His cock still twitched and throbbed, as if at any given moment he would swell and fuck her senseless again.

"My *shuarra*." The heavy vibrations of his voice rumbled against the back of her neck.

"Mmmm, yes," Naomi murmured as she drifted to sleep in his warm arms, not aware of the chill in the air any longer.

CHAPTER
FIVE

NAOMI

Naomi woke with a start. The bed was empty. The cabin was still dark.

It wasn't morning yet ... well, actually it could be. Sunrise in January in this part of Alaska wasn't until nearly ten o'clock.

She inched out of the bed and found her clothes, then her shoes.

"Col?" she called.

No answer.

She rubbed the back of her head where the bandage was wrapped tight. Nothing hurt. Not even a twinge.

Naomi hurried to the bathroom and pulled off the strips of purple fabric. She bent and twisted in front of the mirror enough to see that the wound on the back of her neck was gone. Healed. Just *poof*, it was gone. It hadn't been a terrible cut. But there had been blood. There should at least be a scab. She ran her fingers over the smooth unblemished skin again.

Her bladder clenched, warning her she still needed to get outside and find the outhouse. Getting out here and realizing that everything north of the coastline was a dry cabin—well, not in the city—had been a shock to her city girl disposition. She could handle an outhouse, even in minus thirty-degree temps. It was just a more rustic porta-potty, right?

Her blue coat caught her eye where it'd fallen on the floor next to the sink. She pulled it on and went back out into the main room. Barefoot wasn't going to work. She hunted around, finding one sock under the bed and the other in the far corner of the house.

A giggle slipped from between her lips. Had Col really been in such a hurry that her clothes had *literally* flown around the cabin? One of her rubber snow boots was on the couch. She pulled it on and searched for the other, jumping up and down a little like a toddler in desperate need of a potty break.

"Where the damn hell is my other boot?" Naomi looked down at her sock. No way was she getting her only sock wet in the snow. She clomped around and looked again, finally finding it halfway behind the couch. She rolled her eyes, yanked it from its hiding place and shoved her foot inside. Then she rushed for the front door.

Darkness spread out before her. Not pitch black, thanks to the stars and the northern lights, but still it was creepy-dark for a girl used to the always-bright-never-sleepy city of New York.

At least at the cabin she'd rented north of McKinley Park, she'd had her cellphone and a flashlight. Here, she was totally cut off from the outside.

Naomi squinted and stared into the dark. First the left. Then to the right. A blockish dark form to the right could be it. She stepped out of the safety of the fire-lit cabin and toward the dark blob. "Please be the outhouse."

She crunched through the deep snow, thankful that the resort guide had convinced her to go with the over-the-knee boots.

The dark shape got clearer as she moved closer. Definitely the outhouse.

Her heart slowed, and she released the breath she'd been holding. She was fine. Nothing had eaten her.

She pulled the lever down and opened the door, breathing another sigh of relief at the sight of a plastic tub with toilet paper inside it. Looking for paper inside the cabin hadn't even crossed her mind. Naomi quickly closed the door behind her and relieved herself.

She was pulling up her jeans when a low growl outside made her heart leap out of her chest. "Shit! You scared me, Col." She fastened her pants and pushed open the door. "Can't a girl pee without—"

Another, louder growl blew hot air straight into her face.

A scream ricocheted inside the small building. It took a moment before Naomi realized the high-pitched cry was coming from her. She kicked at the enormous snapping wolf jaws in the opening and yanked the door closed. Her whole body shook as adrenaline rushed through her like a cabbie back home fighting rush hour, giving her enough strength to hold the door closed.

The wolf snarled and clawed at the thick planks of wood. Splinters broke off. It would be only a matter of time before he got to her.

"Col!" She hoped to God the dragon man was close enough to hear her. "Col, help!"

The outhouse rocked.

The wolf was huge.

Bigger than anything she'd ever seen. Bigger than a damn bear.

Tightness clawed at Naomi's lungs. Her heart slammed against the inside of her ribs like a pinball bouncing against bumpers.

The creature was trying to push the entire building over.

"Stop it! Please," she sobbed, hanging onto the lever on the door. It kept trying to swing open.

The outhouse rocked again, lifting her a few inches off the ground before it fell back, jarring her. She lost hold of the door lever and fell to the ground hard in front of the bench in the outhouse.

The door swung open and instead of a wolf, a huge man loomed over her. He was dressed like Col—bare chest, kilt-thing—but it wasn't her dragon man.

This guy was six and a half feet of tall-dark-and-fang-bared monster. If she hadn't been so scared, she might've thought he was attractive with his long black hair and hooded brow, but the menacing golden eyes and the teeth totally stole that opportunity.

"Col!" She screamed again.

The man lunged forward.

She closed her eyes and tensed, waiting for him to pull her out. Waiting for him to hurt her.

But nothing happened.

Instead, there was silence and then *warm* air being blown across her body.

She opened her eyes to an enormous black snout, bigger than the entire outhouse moving toward her. "Holy shit!" Naomi kicked at the giant nostril before her brain registered.

Dragon.

The black dragon chuffed another warm breath over her. Shook his head as if he couldn't believe she'd just kicked him. He flicked his tongue out and moved forward again to nudge her.

"Where's the other guy?" she asked, climbing to her feet and crawling out of the mess of broken planks.

The dragon licked his lips and his dark eyes glowed gold.

"You ate him!" Not that she wasn't grateful. She had almost been attacked herself, but that wolf ... or man. Whatever he was had been trying to kill her. Her gut said she'd be dead if Col hadn't shown up when he did.

Still, it was strange to think that the guy who had saved her was first, a dragon, second, he'd saved her again by *eating* a *person* in what ... one bite?

He moved, nudging her again with his snout.

She patted the ridge of his muzzle and frowned. "I'm not kissing you with people guts in your teeth. Just so you know. How could you eat a person?"

Col shifted a second later. His bare chest illuminated by the starlight and tinted green by the northern lights. He ran his hands up and down her entire body. "Did he touch you? Why are you outside alone?"

"I had to pee." She shivered as he continued to feel up and down her legs and arms. "I'm okay. You got him before he touched me. I'm just a little shook up. That was freaking scary...You ate a person!"

"He was Wolf Tribe, and he was trying to kill you." Like he thought that was a good enough reason to eat a person. "I couldn't burn him. The flame would've hit you too. And I didn't eat him." He pointed off into the scrub. "His body is there. Should I drag it out to show you?"

Relief washed away a tiny bit of the bile in the back of her throat. "So ... you didn't eat a person?"

Col shook his head. "No, I did not eat a person."

Naomi released a long breath and reached up a hand.

"You should've waited for me to return." He growled, ignoring her hand, and instead lifted her off from the ground and carried her back to the cabin door.

"I had to pee. You weren't here, and I couldn't wait."

"I heard you scream and thought they'd found you." The sigh that slipped from his broad chest, made her heart do a flip flop.

"Who? The other dragons?"

He pushed through the door and closed it with his foot. "They are close. I was spreading my scent to the west to keep them away from this cabin. To give you time to heal before we have to move." Col let her down from his arms and helped her sit on the couch. He pulled off her big bulky rubber boots and then covered her with a blanket from the basket next to the hearth. "I brought food. Stay." It was an order. One she didn't mind following. Then, he disappeared back out into the night.

"Better not be chunks of that dude," Naomi called out after his retreating form, somewhat kidding, but there was a part of her that wasn't sure the dragon man wouldn't try to feed her the flesh of his enemies.

He returned a moment later with a large haunch of meat. "It is not the man." A glint of amusement sparkled in his eyes. "Other things will eat him. And the scent of his corpse should keep others from the Wolf Tribe from venturing close."

"Good to know," she answered, pulling the blanket closer. The near-death experience still had her a bit worked up. Just having Col back inside the cabin helped her settle. His presence soothed her in a way she couldn't explain, except that it felt as though she needed to be with him.

Which again brought up feelings of guilt and betrayal. Like her being with Col was hurting Tommy. Which was unfair. She knew it in the back of her mind. She was being unreasonable with herself.

Everyone told her Tommy's death wasn't her fault. Except her own heart. Why couldn't she forgive herself?

Col sat with the leg on the hearth and set up the spit inside it to roast the leg. He'd cut it to fit before he'd brought it inside.

At least she hadn't had to watch him hacking at it or skinning it. Really, it looked just like a roast from the butcher's shop down the street from her apartment back home.

The scent of the meat sizzling over the fire made her stomach rumble noisily.

Col turned to her and smiled. "Good to see the fright didn't scare off your appetite."

"Maybe you could just stay here for a while."

"I will not leave you again tonight *shuarra,* but I had to make sure we were safe here, at least for today."

"Guess the wolves didn't get the memo." She leaned her head against the arm of the couch.

"The wolves are always looking to strike against other tribes. They attacked simply because you are my mate." He moved from the hearth and joined her on the couch. "I thought you would sleep until I returned."

"I missed you." Naomi's feelings bubbled out like a spring before she could think anything through. She cuddled closer to his warm body and pressed her head into the crook of his shoulder.

His chest vibrated, and his arms tightened around her. He kissed the top of her head, pressing down all her wild curls. "I owe Fate for bringing you to me, Naomi."

"I like the way you purr when you're happy."

"I do not purr," he scoffed lightly. "I am not a cat."

"Okay then, you hum," she said, pressing closer.

Col grunted but didn't object again. So, calling the purring noise he made a *hum* must've been acceptable.

"The meat will be done soon."

She rubbed her cheek against his warm skin and dozed off, letting the worry and guilt and everything stewing in her mind disappear into the peaceful sound of Col's heartbeat and the crackle of the fire in the hearth.

From her research, it was uncommon for cabins to have fireplaces, but she was glad the builders had broken the rule this one time.

The smell of the roasting meat was almost like heaven.

CHAPTER
SIX

COL

Col slipped from beneath his sleeping mate and moved to kneel in front of the stone fireplace. He used the small knife at his belt to cut thin slices of the game from the roasted haunch. He'd have to remember to ask her at some point what the antlered deer-like creatures on this world were called.

The savory aroma of the meat filled the cabin and made his mouth water. He hoped his mate would be pleased. He'd eaten the rest of the animal as a dragon and saved the juicy leg to cook and share with her. The fat on the outside had turned clear and had a nice black crisp edge, signaling that it was thoroughly cooked.

He breathed slowly, still trying to assure his dragon, Naomi was safe and sound. He'd been careless, and it'd almost cost him everything. Everything that truly mattered. She was his heart and soul. Without her he would cease to desire life.

The wolf had surely tracked him to the cabin and found his mate. Others would come. It was only a matter of time. He'd told her the dead body would keep them away.

It would. For a while.

Col needed to kill the dragons. He'd never truly have rest until Sefa and Jaha were dead. But he couldn't leave Naomi again.

Hearing her scream earlier had nearly torn his heart from his chest. He'd flown harder than he thought possible to get back to her. He would've died if he hadn't gotten to her in time. His soul would've given up all hope, and he would've prayed for death.

Now he also had to watch for the Wolf Tribe. How many had made it through the portal?

They typically traveled in multi-family packs of ten to fifteen. The male he'd killed outside had been young, probably a scout. They wouldn't miss him for hours, possibly an entire day.

He just needed to feed his mate. She needed her strength to heal and be prepared to travel once the day had dawned.

"Naomi," he said, keeping his voice low.

She opened one brown eye and peeked at him from over the edge of the blanket. Her curls bounced and sprawled over her forehead, giving her a mischievous look.

Col held up a strip of meat and she emerged the rest of the way from the cocoon of the blanket.

"My barbarian barbecues." She covered her mouth to hide her smile and muffle her laughter. Then pushed aside the blanket and moved to sit next to him on the wide hearth.

He didn't understand the joke, but if her humor made her forget the horror she'd experienced because he left her, she could say whatever she liked. Laugh at whatever she pleased.

Eventually he might learn the meanings behind the strange phrases she sometimes used. Until then, he'd be content that she'd accepted him. Cared for him.

Col handed her a piece of meat and watched as she bit into it hungrily. It gave him great pleasure to see her eat and enjoy the food. He waited a moment and gave her another thin strip before taking even one bite for himself.

"This is so good. Thank you." She polished off a second piece. "I don't think I had more than coffee and a granola bar yesterday."

"You must not go outside without me again." He pinned her with his gaze, wishing he was touching her, feeling her softness. The silk of her skin against his.

"I'm not going to just stick to your leg like a helpless baby. You shouldn't feel guilty. You can't control everything that happens to—" Tears welled in her eyes, and she broke visual contact.

"What is wrong, *shuarra*?" He cupped her chin and turned her head to face him. "What saddens you?"

She shook her head free of his touch and wiped her tears with the back of her arm. "It's nothing. Just a memory. I'm fine."

NAOMI

THERE IT WAS. Her guilt over Tommy was connected to the fact that his death was her fault. Was it really?

Yes, she'd needed the medicine. Yes, she'd asked him to pick it up from the pharmacy, but she hadn't been in responsible of the drunk driver in the other car.

It wasn't her fault that man had swung suddenly into oncoming traffic. If she could've saved Tommy, she would've. She knew Col had tried to get to her as fast as he could, but Naomi wouldn't have blamed her death or injury on him if he hadn't made it in time.

Tommy wouldn't blame her for his death.

She could see that now. She could also see that Col would've taken the hit if something had happened to her. He would've blamed himself. Suffered. Just as she had. Naomi couldn't change that ... he loved her.

He really did. In less than twenty-four hours, he'd taken the leap of faith that she belonged to him. With him. Could she care for him the same way?

It'd wrecked her when she'd lost Tommy. Now, the way she felt about Col... She'd let him into her heart. He was a part of her in a way that she couldn't explain. If she lost him like she'd lost Tommy, she wouldn't survive this time.

"Col?" She pulled the blanket up over her shoulders. She wasn't cold, but it made her feel safer. Strange to think a blanket offered protection, but it did.

"Yes, my *shuarra*."

"What else is out there? How did you get to earth?"

"Earth?"

"The name of the planet you're on," Naomi replied. "You didn't know where you were going?"

He shook his head. "The magick-benders had to find a habitable planet. After dozens of tries and years of searching, they found this one only a few days ago. We'd all but given up hope."

"What happened on your world? You haven't really said more than your family died and you followed the two killers here."

"Our world was burning. Volcanos were enveloping the land valley by valley. Our region's magick-bender finally succeeded in opening a portal to escape to here." Col's voice dragged, pain etched deeply on his face. "When I flew through the portal, there were hundreds below me climbing the mountain to escape through its horizon. I've only scented perhaps a couple dozen survivors at the most while I was out earlier."

Tears welled in Naomi's eyes. She couldn't imagine how hard it would be to know the entire world was burning, and that all those people hadn't made it to safety. As strange as it was to think about people from another world sharing hers—people that shifted into large scary predators—her heart hurt for all the lives that had been lost. She knew what loss felt like all too well.

"So other dragons. And now wolves."

Col shook his head. "Lions, bears, at least one tiger too," he said, his voice softening with sadness.

"Wait." She gulped and sat up straight. "You're saying there are lions and tigers in Alaska. Right now?"

"At least a couple."

"Can more of your people still escape?"

He shook his head. "The portal is gone. I passed by where it opened this evening while you still slept."

"Were ... were you thinking of leaving?" Naomi choked out. Just the mere thought made her stomach twist into knots. She'd let herself get attached so quickly.

He called her his mate, and she believed it.

Accepted it. Embraced it even.

"No, *shuarra.* I was merely checking to see if the cowards I hunted had fled back home to escape my wrath. Never fear I would leave. I will be at your side until I draw my last breath." Col joined her on the couch, slipped an arm around her, and pulled her into his side, tucking her head beneath his chin. "You are part of my soul, Naomi."

His warmth soothed her fear. Of course, he wouldn't leave her. But accidents happened.

She needed him to forget about these other dragons. Naomi wanted him to be safe and stay with her.

"So, these *other* shifters, they don't like you?"

"My tribe was at peace with everyone in the valley, except the wolves. The wolves never make peace. They like to fight. To hunt. To kill. They are dangerous and cunning and ruthless."

"Makes sense." She shivered, especially after what she'd encountered this morning. "There are real wolves out here too. How will we tell the difference between your people and just a plain wolf?"

"You saw how large he was?"

Naomi shuddered. "He was seriously the size of a dire wolf on the Game of Thrones miniseries."

"I do not know the animal you speak of, but all Reylean wolves will be that large."

Her mouth dropped. "Not good."

"Now you see why I do not want you to leave the cabin alone," he said. "My bite made you ill. You have a head injury. We will stay a few more hours. At least until the sun rises. The dead body will keep other wolves away. I threw my scent all the way to the other side of the mountain. The dragons will not find us. You are safe." Col nuzzled her curls and kissed the top of her head.

"You know the fever is gone, and so is my head injury. Even the cut on the back of my head disappeared like magic." Naomi brushed her fingers over the place at the base of her skull that should've a long gash in it. "And if we wait until the sun rises, won't the other dragons see you?"

He tugged her into his lap. "I must finish them, Naomi. Now that they know I am here, they will hunt me as I hunt them." His hands slipped to the back of her neck and his eyes widened. "You healed quickly."

"You're not kidding; I should still have a mark or a scab or something. But it's like it never happened."

"Your people do not typically heal at this rate?" His gaze drove through her like a white-hot poker. His hands slipped down to her hips.

Naomi tried not to let her mind wander to how much she enjoyed the way he looked at her, touched her and...

Ohmygod. Just stop.

"Not usually, no," she finally managed. It was taking all her willpower not to grind herself against him.

Seriously, it was like she was in heat. Or just starved for sex and affection.

Two years of celibacy could do that to a girl. Or it was just Col. She was pretty convinced it was the latter. There was just something about him that made her *hungry*.

His eyes narrowed, and a smile curved the corners of his mouth. "My *shuarra* has needs." He leaned closer, invading her space, his gaze trailing to her mouth and down to her covered breasts. One corner of his mouth quirked up into a full-on smirk.

Her core throbbed traitorously.

Get a grip, Naomi.

"We should get ready to leave. I need to get back to my stuff and—" her words were cut off by his mouth covering hers.

His tongue prodded insistently, until it gained entry. Followed by an assault on her mouth that left her completely breathless.

Their tongues lashed frantically against each other, as if there were only moments to live, and then he switched to slow languid thrusts and strokes that made every square inch of Naomi's body hum with a hunger she couldn't ignore.

She was lost.

Consumed by her need for Col.

Her dragon man buried his hands in her hair and laid her back on the couch. He pulled her close and pinned her down in the same breath.

Naomi clawed at his shoulders, scraping her fingers down the hard, rippling muscles of his back. She reached and cupped his tight ass through the leather and fabric of his kilt, pressing her hips up and against his hardness. Heat seared her body like a wildfire burning out of control. The ferocity of the kiss grew.

He pawed at her clothes, pulling them off between pants and breaths of desperation. In moments, they were both naked again.

Lips to lips. Skin to skin.

Her hands couldn't get enough of touching him.

His were the same on her. First her breasts. Then he stroked her hip. Then he wrapped his hands around her thighs, pulling them open.

He slid home with one forceful stroke.

Naomi cried out, nearly coming just from the fullness. "Please, Col." She bit back a whimper. She'd been so close, but now he was moving excruciatingly slowly, drawing out her pleasure, keeping her just far enough from the edge that she couldn't climax.

"What does my mate desire?"

"More. Make me feel more," she moaned into his mouth as he swept her lips again and moved to nibbling down the side of her neck.

She clenched around him, her body begging to be taken harder. Begging to feel the pleasure only he could give her.

When they were together it was like the rest of the world faded away. Naomi could feel how much he cared for her. Feel the walls around his heart coming down at the same time hers were crumbling to dust, allowing him to see more of her. All of her.

She pushed into his thrusts, matching move for move.

Faster and faster. Harder. Deeper.

Naomi buried her face in Col's neck and arched her hips, drawing him even closer.

He growled in her ear and nipped at her shoulder. Not a bite this time, but it reminded her of the mark he'd given her that sealed their mating.

She still didn't quite understand it, but she wanted him.

Above everything else in the world, he was now the most important person.

Col turned just slightly, giving himself room to slip a hand between their sweat slicked bodies. His fingers brushed her clit and Naomi's pants went ragged and she whimpered, as her release rushed toward her with the fury of a hurricane.

"Col, oh God, I'm—" Her body rippled and spasmed around his cock, as blinding pleasure coursed through her veins. She writhed in his arms, but he didn't give an inch. A scream tore from her throat, and she dug her fingers into his arms. She bit down on his shoulder and continued to cry out as the first orgasm rolled into the second.

He roared, joining her on the climax.

She felt his warm seed filling her, making her slicker, as Col continued to pound into her until his movements slowly stuttered and came to a grinding halt.

His weight pressed her down into the couch, and they lay there panting and sated. Naomi wished nothing would ever change.

Col rolled to the side, putting her back against the back of the couch, pinning her without being on top of her. His cock was still inside her, pulsing and twitching every so often as if it had a mind of its own and wasn't at all done with her.

She laid a leg over his hip and wiggled.

He shoved his hips harder against hers so that she could barely move.

She peered over at him in the lowlight of the fire from the hearth.

His brown eyes were golden. Molten.

"You do not fear my dragon," he said, a pleased hum in his tone. He nuzzled her face and placed light kisses on her cheek and forehead and then one right on the tip of her nose.

"Why would I fear something that cares for me?"

"That loves you," Col corrected, his voice breathy.

"That loves me," she repeated. How did they skip over the get-to-know-you part and straight to the hearts-are-locked-as-one part?

He stroked in and out of her swollen sex and she couldn't help but moan in pleasure.

She chuckled, "I get that you *make* love to me, but actually *love*? You don't know me."

There had to be a catch, a caveat to the fantasy-dragon-man and his soulmate stuff.

"When I saw you lying in the snow, your soul glowed for me. I abandoned my mission, because I couldn't leave you there. You were mine. I needed you more than I needed anything else, even justice for my family."

"I don't remember looking any different."

"You are not Reylean. I don't think you can *see* magick. But I can. Fate marked you. Your soul glowed like a flame from inside your body. Only a fated mate can see that kind of magick," he said, stroking a little faster. His cock had swelled again, stretching and filling her so full that Naomi could barely think past the pleasure of his touch.

"When my soul reached out to yours, I knew nothing mattered more than you. If I abandoned you, Fate might decide to take back her gift. I couldn't risk losing you, even if it meant the other dragons had to die another day."

He reached between her slick folds and stroked until a dam broke inside. The world rushed around Naomi as she climaxed again. She heard him groan. Felt him come.

She just kept sailing higher and higher. Her body pulsed like it'd been struck by a lightning bolt.

Everything tingled and burned—in a good way.

"You are my *shuarra*, Naomi. There will be no other for as long as we both draw breath."

A cry tore from her chest and she let her head fall against his breastbone. "I'm just a woman, a selfish, broken woman who's been hiding from the world for the last two years. How can I be your soul mate? How can you know for sure? I mean, I feel so good when we're together, but it's been so long since I let a man touch me. I think I may just be starved for affection. I isolated myself after —" Tears poured down her cheeks. Her lungs gasped for air between the cries. "It was my fault I lost him. And it will be my fault when I lose you too."

All the guilt and pressure of the last two years came crashing down. She'd thought she'd put it behind her. She'd thought she'd made the choice to start over, but really, she'd just slammed the door on that part of her ragged soul and tried to say she was over it.

"Who did you lose, *shuarra*?"

Naomi shook her head, sucking in a quick breath. How could she talk about Tommy with Col? He'd hate her or resent her or think that she was still in love with Tommy.

Was she? Was she incapable of moving on?

He pulled his cock out of her and a profound sense of loneliness overwhelmed her.

Col would leave her. Just like Tommy had. Something would steal him away, and she'd be alone again.

A moment later his fingers parted her wet folds and slid inside her.

Naomi drew air into her shuddering lungs. "W-what are you doing?"

"Reminding you, you are mine. That you are not alone. Even if my cock is not inside you, nothing has changed *shuarra*. Your body. Your soul. We are bound for life. If you need to feel me inside you to remind you of that, I am more than willing. Now, tell me who you lost?"

"I can't." Her voice broke with the weight of the pain bearing down on her like she was carrying the car Tommy had died in on her back.

His fingers curled inside her, drawing a gasp of pleasure.

"Tell me," he ordered, his voice firmer this time. "I can feel every part of your soul, Naomi. I can feel the broken parts and the whole parts. The sad and tired places and the places where you cling to happiness. Tell me who you lost. Let him go, Naomi. For yourself. For us."

"I thought I had." Her voice broke as the pain gushed to the surface. "I thought I'd made peace with it after you marked me. I'd closed the door on that part of my life. I wanted you. I wanted to be happy with you. I buried him."

Col's chest rumbled next to her. It wasn't an angry growl, but more a soothing purr ... or hum as he preferred it to be named. "You must tell me."

"What if I lose you?" The fear stabbed at her like a dagger of ice straight into the heart.

"You will not," he said, as if it weren't an option.

Could she trust that? If she told him about Tommy, would he still look at her like she was the only woman he would ever look at? Would he still want her for always?

He slipped his fingers from her core and cupped her face instead.

Col pulled her face up just a little, so she had to meet his gaze.

God, those golden eyes were her kryptonite. The way he looked at her. Like she was the center of his universe.

Only one other man had ever looked at her that way.

"Tommy died because of me," Naomi said, her voice hollow and filled with pain. "I loved him, and he died because of me. I was sick, and he went to get medicine. It was so late and dark, and a drunk driver hit his car. He died because of me." She cried through the words, but she got them out. It was what Col wanted, and she wanted to do what he'd asked of her, even if it meant that look in his eyes went away. "We were supposed to get married. Have babies. Grow old together. And I lost him. He left me."

Her dragon man kept holding her. Kept staring. His gaze hadn't wavered. Hadn't changed. He just waited. Like he knew there was more.

There was.

"It was my fault. Everyone told me it wasn't, but it *was*. And then I met you and you said those things about losing me earlier, and for a moment I thought I'd let it go. I thought I'd put the pain behind me and let Tommy go. But every time I think about what you still have to do. You have to hunt those dragons. Now there are wolves out there that hate you. And what am I going to do if I lose you too? I think it might kill me, and then I feel guilty all over again, because how is it fair that I get to fall in love again and Tommy is gone?"

All the pain and pent-up years of self-loathing and guilt and torture came bubbling up to the surface and just kept spilling out into words.

"And I don't want to lose you. I don't want to be alone again." She gasped for breath and her whole body shuddered.

"I can't promise you a certain number of years, *shuarra*. No one can. The man you loved died caring for you. There is no greater honor for a mate. I would die doing the same without a second thought. We can only live the time we have, but we can't be happy if we're always thinking this moment might be the last. Would your Tommy want you to be in pain? If it'd been *you* that died, would you deny him happiness and wish him to always be sick for you?"

Naomi shook her head.

"I'm going to try something." He released her face and leaned back so that there was a little space between their bodies. "It is very old. I do not know if the magick will work in this world. I'm not a magick-bender, but this ceremony is part of Reylean custom when mates find each other."

She watched as he put his finger to his mouth and pricked it with one of his fangs. Blood ran down his finger and Naomi swallowed but didn't speak.

Col pressed the bloody finger to her collarbone and drew a symbol.

She couldn't tell what. Something from his world.

Then he drew it on his chest as well.

He spoke a phrase of something she couldn't understand. Over and over, he chanted.

Each time he finished, her body grew warmer. The fire she'd felt right after he'd bitten her returned tenfold.

She cried out, and then gasped. Light poured from her chest and his. It filled the space between them with a beautiful soft glow.

Naomi's breath caught. Then it hit. The love he felt for her. The dedication. The kindness and caring that made him who he was.

Then the anger and drive for justice he felt was necessary so that his parents and family would find peace.

All of it.

She could feel every day of joy he'd had. Every day of sorrow. Every achievement. Every loss. In the midst of everything, she could feel how she now lay planted like a hundred-year-old willow tree right at the center.

She was at his core now.

He was hers.

Everything she felt in his soul ... in his heart.

He could feel hers just the same.

She'd loved Tommy completely and wholly, but she'd never known the depths of his soul, never felt his every hope and dream and heartache.

Col had allowed her to see a part of himself that no one else had ever seen and would never see again.

He was right. Now that she'd told him about Tommy, it was like the dark secret of his death had been set free. She wasn't chained to the memory. Wasn't afraid it would come out and ruin what'd been formed between her and Col.

She would always love Tommy, and that was okay. Now, she could love Col and move forward with her life with him, too.

"I love you, Col," she said, her voice shaky, but determined.

The light between their bodies slowly faded as each soul returned to its place.

The warmth filled her with a peace she hadn't felt in so long.

Col's arms wrapped tightly around her, and she took a deep peaceful breath.

"And I love you, *shuarra*. Sleep now, my beautiful mate." He nuzzled her curls with his lips. "Be free."

CHAPTER
SEVEN

NAOMI

Sunlight streamed in the front window of the cabin, giving the large room a bright glow. Col was already up. He'd doused the fire, cleaned up, and disposed of the leftover food.

Her clothes were folded neatly at the foot of the bed and her boots were standing next to the end of the couch.

They had to leave. This cabin belonged to other people who could come back any time. They'd already used some of their precious water supply. Naomi felt guilty for not having anything to leave in exchange.

"Did you sleep well, *shuarra*?" Col asked, his gaze falling on her as he entered the cabin and stomped his snow-covered boots on the rug. "Everything is ready to go."

She slithered out of the bed and pulled on her clothes one piece at a time. Strangely the cabin didn't feel too cold, even with the fire out. She pulled on her long wool socks and traipsed across the room to the couch. "How are we getting back to my stuff?"

"I will shift and carry you," Col answered, dropping into the seat next to her.

Naomi's stomach bottomed out, a whole different fear coming to roost. "Ummm, that doesn't really sound pleasant." Heights weren't something she handled well. In the back of her mind, she recalled he'd flown her here. But to get back, she been hoping for ... what? "Maybe we could just walk." Her mouth dried instantly. Her hands became clammy, even in the biting cold. Fear clambered aboard her mind like an old friend who knew they would never be left behind.

"I would never drop you."

"I get that, but it's just. I'm ... well ... I'm afraid of heights," she said, tugging her other boot on.

Col slipped an arm around her shoulders and pulled her close. "The sooner the battle is fought, the sooner it can be won."

"Are you talking about your battle with the dragons or mine with puking from being up too high?"

He chuckled and rose from the couch, pulling her along with him. "Both." He took her puffy blue coat down from the peg by the door and handed it to her.

She put it on and zipped it up, like somehow it was armor for what she was about to do. Was she really going to allow a dragon to carry her as he flew through the air?

Yes. Granted, it was Col. She trusted him. But still. Carry her? In the sky. High above everything?

Yes.

Her stomach fluttered and a small, still voice in the

back of her mind soothed her fear. She was his mate. His *shuarra,* as he so liked to call her.

He'd never put her in harm's way. Naomi could do this. They really did need to get out of this cabin before the owners showed up and threatened them or pressed charges for breaking and entering. The last thing she needed was Col to be put in jail.

What if he got angry and lost his temper? Could he control his dragon?

So many questions.

"Are you ready?"

She took a deep breath and released it. "No, not really," she said without thinking.

He smiled and walked to her, wrapping his strong arms around her body, making her feel small and safe and loved. How he did that with just a hug, she'd never know.

It happened. Every single time.

"You will be safe, Naomi."

She took another deep, fortifying breath to still her nerves and her overactive brain that'd possibly flashed half a billion ways this scenario could go wrong.

Col went out the door, glancing over his shoulder to make sure she was following.

Naomi stopped on the steps of the cabin.

He was already out about twenty feet into the clearing. One moment he was a man and the next he was a dragon. A winged black fantasy creature, with a body the size of a Mac truck.

His black scales shone like they were made of onyx stone. His wings unfurled and stretched above her like a canopy of black leather. After a few shakes he tucked them close to his sides.

His head was rimmed with several long horns that curled back over his neck, almost creating a protective plate like a triceratops. The spikes continued along his back, several rows of yardstick sized spears, that tapered off in a heavily spiked tail that reminded Naomi of a medieval war weapon, except ten times bigger than anything a person would try to lift. Hell, one of his muscular legs was the size of her entire body.

Col lowered his elongated neck and shoved his nose toward her, nudging her hand gently until she rubbed him right above the lips that covered a row of teeth as long as her legs. She'd touched him in this form before ... well, she hadn't really been that conscious last time.

So, this really counted as the *first* time. Her brain still couldn't truly wrap around the fact that he was *real*.

A real fucking dragon.

"Wait. Shift back," she said, staying in the doorway. His clothes hadn't shredded or anything. They just sort of disappeared and reappeared when he needed them.

Col's dragon morphed in an instant and he was standing before her, clothed in his kilt and boots, and looking sexier than the latest Conan the Barbarian movie character.

"How do your clothes stay intact? Your dragon is huge. But when you shift, you don't destroy them."

He tapped the side of his arm where a leather band was wrapped around a couple of times.

She'd seen it before but hadn't really paid much attention.

"The magick-benders in my world make charms for us." Col turned to show her the carved bone amulet tied tightly to his arm.

"So, if you lose the charm..."

"I would lose the ability to shift with clothing." He raised an eyebrow. "Should I take it off?"

Heat rushed her face. She wouldn't mind the view but didn't want anyone else taking a peek. "No, I think it's better on."

"Less distracting?" he asked, the hint of a smile curving his lips.

"We'll go with that, yes," she answered. "I'm ready ... I think. Well, maybe not."

Col shifted again, then lumbered a few steps closer before reaching out with a front claw and scooping her up from the ground.

She clung to one of the claw-like fingers as he brought her close to his chest.

He waited for her to calm, then tightened his hold.

She felt secure, even though her heart was bashing her ribs like a wild animal caught in a cage. Her breath came in pants. Naomi probably should close her eyes, but the truth was, she wanted to see what Col saw.

Maybe just this once she could forget her paralyzing fear of heights.

He used his other front claw to move a pile of the wood stack in front of the door he'd broken. It wasn't perfect, but at least it would hopefully deter wildlife from trying to get the door open.

Snow swirled around them as Col pumped his wings and launched himself into the air.

She peered down between the claws that held her tightly. They flew higher and higher, until the cabin was toy-sized below them. A rush of cold wind burned her face and Naomi was suddenly grateful for Col's warmth on her back. The bitterness of the wind on the ground was nothing compared to the icy blades of the air at this altitude, but the landscape was amazing. She wished she had her camera.

He banked and turned suddenly.

Oh God!

She barely contained the screech of fright. Clamped her eyes shut and tried to think of happy things. Her family. Her camera. Col. She was safe with him. He had her. Everything was fine.

Except you are flying over the Alaskan wild in the claws of a dragon.

Naomi forced herself to breathe. Her heart rate slowed just a little.

Col's flight evened out and he dipped a little lower.

Slowly she opened her eyes again. She didn't recognize the clearing at first. She spotted the tripod with her camera still standing beneath a lone pine and the bright blue cover still neatly wrapped over the snowmachine. At least everything still looked intact. She wouldn't lose her deposit on the rental.

He circled the clearing a few times before landing softly on the pure white spread of powder. He set her down and shifted to his human form to help her off the ground.

Naomi stood and brushed the snow off her pants. Her legs wobbled just a little. The sensation and adrenaline from the flight still coursed through her veins like a jolt of caffeine.

She looked over her shoulder into the trees where she'd fled from the first two dragons and couldn't help the shudder of fear that prickled up and down her spine.

She clomped over to her camera set up beneath a large single pine. It'd been sheltered from the weather by the low hanging branches. Probably some elk had checked it out, but otherwise it looked untouched.

Naomi unscrewed it from the tripod and tucked it into the small bag hanging from a branch. Then untied the ropes she'd used to anchor the tripod. Once everything was packed and wrapped and secure in the other, larger bag she'd left—also hanging in the tree, she returned to where Col was standing in the center of the clearing.

His eyes were flickering gold, meaning his dragon was close to the surface.

"What's wrong?"

He didn't answer. Instead, she was covered in a spray of snow, snatched from the ground by a giant claw and tucked once more against his warm scaly black chest.

A frightening call echoed through the sky like a sound effect from a Jurassic Park movie. Then another.

Then Col's chest vibrated and answered with his own body-shaking-pee-in-your-pants scream or trumpet or whatever a dragon noise was called.

Naomi clung to his claws and tried not to puke or wet herself. Her bag of camera equipment was on the ground. Not that it was particularly important if she was about to be flambéed alive or eaten by a dragon.

Two dragons, one black and the other red, rose above the ridge just ahead. They were rapidly approaching, and Col was *pissed*.

Growls rumbled from his chest. His wings pumped hard, and he rose higher and higher.

The other dragons were big, but not as large as Col. Still, it was two against one. That couldn't be good.

They were climbing now too and rapidly catching up.

Why wasn't Col rising anymore?

It seemed like he was waiting. Hovering.

Fire blasted from the black dragon's mouth into the air.

Then the red added flame to the mix. They both screamed the spine-tingling bugle call again.

No mistake. They were out for blood.

Col's wings flattened against his back. Everything seemed to drop at once.

The feeling of weightlessness made Naomi's stomach rise into her throat. She couldn't breathe. Her heart felt as though it stopped.

The ground shot toward them.

They were almost on top of the rising two dragons.

Holy fucking shit!

EIGHT

COL

Col dropped toward the attackers. Battle strategy said he had to take one of them out of the fight immediately. He couldn't protect Naomi against two dragons. Wasn't foolish enough to think he could.

His only choice was knock Sefa from the sky and give himself enough time to kill Jaha. He could hunt the female later.

His mate had gone stiff in his right claw, but she wasn't fighting. At least surrounded on most sides by his body she was protected, should the murderer throw fire in his direction. The flame would blind him temporarily, but not injure him like it would Naomi.

The traitors didn't have time to try and burn his mate. Col had risen above their line of sight. They'd get no warning.

Neither of the enemy dragons would expect him to

drop on them. It was dangerous to tuck the wings and fall like he was. Getting wings back open after a dead drop was one of the hardest maneuvers ever mastered by dragon warriors.

He bent his head just before impact, and let his left shoulder collide with the female's back. Bones crunched beneath her hide. Col hoped at least one of her wing joints had been crushed.

The scream she released made him roar an angry response.

She'd been part of the murder of his family. Of his whole tribe.

Her cry reminded him of the pain he'd heard in his sister Kela's voice, as the great stone boulders the traitors had thrown from the sky had crushed her legs. She'd shifted, but her back had been broken. And even her dragon was able to do nothing more than drag itself along on the ground, trying to find cover. Then another rock had crushed the side of Kela's head. She'd dropped dead no more than thirty paces from him.

Jaha and the others had been prepared. They'd all thrown the boulders at once. All with deadly aim. Most of his family had died instantly. They'd been out in the open, helping their tribe prepare for the exodus.

No one had been ready for an attack.

Not even him.

The falling ash and volcanic rocks were like meteors and made it dangerous for their wings. All patrols had been grounded. Everyone's energy and focus had been on organizing and joining the other tribes on the trek up the mountain to the waiting portal. All disagreements and territory wars had been set aside. Survival had united the valley.

Or so they'd thought.

Col's father had put him in charge of the elders at the back of the group. His great grandmother had shifted beside him before he'd seen the burning rocks barreling down to crush them both. He should've been watching better. He should've done something. He shouldn't have let his guard down.

The collision with Sefa's body slowed his descent. He fought the wind and sheer and managed to open his wings.

Jaha's sister fell like a rock to the snowy ground below.

His victory was short-lived. Flames spread across Col's back like a warm summer breeze. He twisted in the air, letting his spikes and wings take the brunt of the heat.

Naomi was safe. He could feel her heart pounding against his chest. Her small hands clung to his claws like talons themselves.

He trumpeted a challenge to Jaha, and whirled to face him, spraying fire with the cry. The flames brightly burned, blinding the enemy male for the moment Col needed. He pumped his wings and reached out with his back feet.

His claws found a hold on the softer scales of Jaha's underbelly. He contracted them and ripped away huge chunks of the younger dragon's hide.

The black dragon warrior cried out in agony but didn't give up. His fate was to kill or be killed.

Col would allow no other outcome.

More memories flooded back as his rage boiled in his veins. Jaha and his father's group of exiled dragons had broken the treaty of Exodus Day. They'd murdered innocents. They'd not engaged in a battle like honorable warriors, instead they'd carried out a massacre against all. Mothers. Children. The elders. All had perished within a matter of a few seconds.

Col was the only son of the royal house of Li'Vhram left alive.

He would avenge his tribe.

Jaha would die.

So would Sefa, if she did not already breathe her last on the ground below them.

He remembered so distinctly the sound of breaking bones and tearing flesh. The way the first boulder had crushed his great grandmother's wings. She'd covered him with her large body, pinning him down in his two-legged form for several moments. By the time he shifted and crawled from beneath her heavy, white-scaled body, the attack had been over.

All members of his tribe were dead or dying.

Col had leapt upon the closest attacker in a rage—a male he recognized as having been exiled from the tribe over a year ago. The male—Jaha's father—had been looting the dying and dead's belongings. Honorless traitor.

Jaha's father had been the first male he'd torn limb from limb. With the rival's blood fresh in his mouth, he'd continued to tear through the others who didn't flee fast enough.

The black dragon and his sister were the only ones

that'd fled toward the portal. The other traitors had flown into the ash and smoke and fire-filled sky to the south of the valley. Reylea would burn them for him.

He'd followed Jaha and Sefa. Col refused to allow them to escape to a new world, where their crimes would go unpunished. Now the time had come for the battle between them to be finished. It would've been over already, had he not come across Naomi, but now that he had her, Col couldn't imagine a life without her.

Jaha threw flame and twisted in the sky, ducking beneath him. The young warrior sought the same vulnerability—his belly.

Col banked hard and the dragon's claws merely glanced off the hard spikes along his back. The young black dragon roared in frustration.

He used the moment to twist in the air and bite at Jaha's leg. Bones crunched in his jaws. Blood flowed through his teeth. The traitor would die a long, slow, and torturous death.

Jaha screamed and yanked his mangled leg free of Col's mouth.

They banked and turned and circled each other for a few seconds before Jaha charged in again.

Stupid youngling.

Col leaned to the right, avoiding the charge and swung his tail hard, ripping a long tear through one of Jaha's wings. It didn't cripple him completely, but he now had to work twice as hard to stay in the air.

More bellows of pain. More sprays of fire.

Each time, Col turned and blocked the flame with his

back and wings. He listened for Naomi's heart. It was steady. Her breathing slow and relaxed. She'd passed out.

Probably for the best.

At least holding her, he was assured that nothing attacked her on the ground while he fought.

Kill. Finish him. His dragon trumpeted the challenge call.

Jaha swung around and tried again for his belly with back claws, but at the last moment twisted in the air. The youngling bit down on Col's tail and pulled hard.

The momentum caught Col off guard. He spread his wings wide and pumped furiously to keep from dropping into a freefall.

The young dragon yanked again and then released with a spray of fire that bathed Col's entire belly and chest in flame.

No!

There was no time to maneuver. No way to block the fire.

Naomi couldn't have survived. Her skin wasn't like his.

Without dragon magick, the super-heated air alone would've killed her with one breath. His heart pounded. He'd lost his *shuarra*.

He'd failed to protect her from a pathetic cowardly youngling who'd *again* targeted an innocent.

His woman. His mate.

He dove at the dragon with an enraged roar. Col bathed the young warrior with flame and found his target within seconds. His jaws clamped down on Jaha's neck.

His back claws raked down the black one's stomach, ripping his softer belly to shreds.

Blood coated his claws. The smell only drove Col's dragon harder.

Jaha screamed, then choked and coughed.

They tumbled through the sky, a mass of wings and claws and blood. He bit down harder, relishing the sound of bones crunching and Jaha's life ebbing away with one last wheezing gasp.

Col released the dead dragon and leapt upward from the body, pushing himself into the sky. The thud of the other dragon's form reverberated through the open clearing. His wings pumped harder and then slowed, easing himself down to land beside the broken and bloody carcass of his enemy.

His frame shook and shivered as he drew in huge lungfuls of air. He still had his right claw clutched tightly to his chest.

Naomi's body.

His dragon couldn't concentrate. All it saw was blood. All it smelled was death and ash. It wanted to rip into Jaha's body and tear it to shreds.

Col needed to see his mate. Needed to know for sure if he'd lost her. He pushed and clawed at the dragon's consciousness.

Shuarra. Our shuarra! he screamed inside his mind. Finally, the dragon relented, giving up control.

He tucked his wings against his large, scaled body and backed away from the gore of Jaha's carcass. He unfolded his claw and let Naomi slide gently out onto the snow. Her beautiful curls hid part of her face. Her skin looked undamaged. Actually, none of her looked damaged. He took a deep breath, slowing his own racing, pounding heartbeat so that he could listen for hers.

Col shuddered out a breath and fell to the ground beside her in his two-legged form.

She was alive. Her heart still beat. She breathed.

How had his claw shielded her?

He'd felt the heat. It'd covered him. Covered *her*. How was her hair not singed? Her skin not blistered and red? She was human and vulnerable, not Reylean. Not dragon. She winced when she touched anything hot. But there she was.

Undamaged. Alive. A beautiful sight cradled by pure white snow. His *shuarra* lived.

A bugle cry sounded from across the clearing.

Col snarled, shifting in an instant and stepping over Naomi to shield her from Sefa.

However, the female dragon didn't turn. She rose slowly into the air and limped away, barely able to fly. Her wing wasn't broken, but it'd been wrenched out of place.

He roared into the air. His dragon wanted more blood. *He* wanted more blood. But Sefa would wait. He'd let her go off to lick her wounds. Then he would hunt her down and end her too.

Justice would be served for his house. For his tribe.

Naomi was his only focus until the scent of another Reylean shifter wafted closer on the cold breeze. Lions were approaching. He swung his head into the wind and breathed deeply. It was strong and close.

They were beyond stupid to come at him when his mate was vulnerable. He'd just dismembered another dragon. The bloody carcass lay not ten feet from him. Did they not value their lives? Did they not think he would end them with one breath of his fire?

Col trumpeted another call, warning them off. Focusing on the trees, he waited and watched. He was exhausted from the fight.

His muscles trembled and shook from exertion, but he wasn't too tired to lay waste to a lion. Or several.

He breathed in deeply. In and out. In and out. Then continued to wait.

CHAPTER
NINE

NAOMI

C old water trickled down her neck. Her hair felt damp too. Col was close, she could feel his presence. She didn't have to open her eyes to confirm it. He was there.

The world had stopped swinging from side to side. She was on the ground again, although her stomach still felt as though it were swaying back and forth and up and down. Everything rumbled, and she rolled quickly, heaving the contents of her stomach all over the white snow.

Naomi opened her eyes, and it took several moments for her vision to clear. White ground beneath her. Check. Trees in the distance. Check. Movement above her made her gulp for a breath. She could smell blood and char, and something else.

A rumble sounded next to her, and an enormous nose nudged her hip.

She nearly screamed in fright before she realized it was Col—as a dragon. Naomi rubbed her mouth with her sleeve and then looked up at him.

He was covered in blood. His face. His wings. A long ugly slice ran down his side.

"You're hurt." She tried to stand too quickly and plopped back down on the snow, her head swirling. "What happened? Are you okay? Are they coming back?"

The dragon nudged her again and stepped closer, nearly putting her beneath his chest. A low growl rumbled, and he swung his head out toward the trees to their left.

Two figures were approaching. They wore the same kilt-looking thing Col did in his human form, except the fabric of theirs wasn't purple. It was brown. They smelled different too. Not like a dragon.

Wait?

Why could she smell them? That was strange.

Naomi lifted her face into the breeze and inhaled deeply. She could, though. She could smell that they were ... *animal.* But they didn't smell like Col. So, what kind of Reylean were they? "Col, who is it?" she asked, reaching out to touch his nearest leg.

He chuffed out a breath.

Naomi could feel his pulse in his leg. It was racing. His leg was trembling too. He was breathing harder than normal.

The fight had taken a lot out of him. He wasn't going to shift back to human form for her because he thought he might have to fight again.

One of the approaching bare-chested men raised a

hand in greeting. He let loose a string of words she didn't understand. She crawled out from under Col and attempted to stand at his side, but his dragon wouldn't have it. His big nose knocked her into the snow again and he sidestepped, putting her right back under his chest.

Fine. She sighed and settled herself against Col's leg— the inside of his leg.

The men continued to approach.

Col seemed to have settled a little after the man spoke, but he still wasn't taking any chances.

Naomi glanced to her right and nearly puked again. The body of a black dragon lay gutted and ripped to shreds not ten feet away.

The snow was stained a deep red all around his lifeless corpse. She'd been awake for the very first part of the fight. Then all the twisting and turning and dropping had quickly sent her into a blackout. She didn't remember anything until just a few minutes ago when she'd awoken on the snow.

She looked up. The two men were closer now. Definitely dressed like Col, with the whole barbarian barechested-kilt-wearing look. The tattoos on their arms were similar to her dragon's, but not quite the same design. These two men had light golden blond hair and blue eyes, a stark contrast to Col's dark hair and dark eyes. No family resemblance whatsoever.

"You know he breathes fire, right?" she called.

The dragon above her coughed, and his chest rumbled.

She could've sworn it sounded like a laugh. If dragons could laugh.

The men paused where they were and looked at each other, then looked back at her. "You are human? From this world?" Now they were speaking English, instead of the strange language they'd spoken at the beginning.

"Yep."

"But you scent as Dragon Tribe," the one on the left spoke up again.

I scent as Dragon Tribe?

Honestly, that didn't surprise her. She and Col had literally spent most of their time in bed together. She'd taken multiple showers, but still, even *she* thought she smelled like Col.

"I'm his mate. That could have something to do with it."

Both men's eyes widened with surprise. "A mate? But you are human? From this world?"

"Yep, already answered that question." Naomi crawled out from under Col's slimy blood-covered chest.

He'd stopped trembling and shaking, but still hadn't shifted back. So, either he didn't want to talk to the others, or he just hadn't decided they weren't a threat yet.

She didn't get the sense they were dangerous. More curious than anything. She stayed right next to Col, regardless of her own sense. She trusted him to protect her.

No matter what.

"Did you glow?"

"Glow?" Naomi asked, her voice rising just a little. "I don't know what you're talking about. Who are you?"

"Forgive us," the man on the left spoke again. His long

blond hair had several narrow braids on either side of his face, keeping his hair out of the way. The braids had leather strips and feathers braided into them as well. His face was well proportioned with a strong nose and a squared off jaw. His blue eyes were bright and reminded her of the ocean on a tropical postcard. "My name is Saul."

"Naomi." Her answer was quick, unhesitant.

He gestured to his companion.

The other man nodded and spoke. "My name is Kann. We are both from the Lion Tribe from the N'ra Lowlands. Same as your mate." His hair was long as well, but shaved on the sides, also blond, but gathered into a series of ponytails and tiny braids that looked to trail about midway down his back. No cords and feathers for this guy.

He definitely pulled off the Viking look. She'd seen trailers for that History Channel TV show, and this guy could've seriously walked right off the set. They both could.

"Nice to meet you, I guess." She spoke slowly, keeping an eye on Col. "You know Col?"

He was still eyeing them as if he hadn't decided whether or not to crush them with his claw or flambé them where they stood. Her mate didn't trust them, and he wasn't about to let his guard down.

It made her feel all warm and gooey inside. And horny.

Geeze. Not now.

She stopped looking at her dragon and turned back to face the other two Reylean men.

"Everyone knows Col of House Li'Vhram, heir of the Dragon Lord of the N'ra Lowlands."

Heir of the what?

Naomi flashed a glance at Col and narrowed her gaze. He'd been holding out on her. "We'll talk about this later, Heir of the Dragon Lord." Her words were laced with surprise and curiosity. What else didn't she know?

Dragon Col snorted out a breath of hot air but didn't take his attention from the two men.

"Why does your dragon hunt other Reyleans?" Kann spoke again.

My dragon.

She liked the sound of that.

Col huffed another angry breath and took a menacing step toward the two men.

Naomi put a hand on his shoulder, trying to avoid the huge smears of blood. "Hey, they just want to make sure you're not going to attack them."

He swung his head around and nudged her shoulder, pushing her closer to him and rumbling like an overgrown happy house cat.

"Right?" she asked, turning her focus back to the other two men.

They both nodded. "We've gathered together a few of the refugees at a cabin closer to a small village called Mystery. The natives have a long unpronounceable name for it, but one woman told us most just called it Mystery," said Kann. He seemed to be more of a talker than his buddy, Saul.

"*Tukisinangitok,*" she rattled off with a smile. She'd researched the small town before arriving. "It's the Native name. In English it translates to Mystery, or hidden place."

"We were hoping the dragons would agree to come with us. There are so few. It would be easier to make a start of it together," Kann continued. "We are a tribal people. Even though most of us lost everyone..."

"You're trying to build a new tribe with those that survived." Naomi's voice stayed soft. Empathy built in her breast like a rising tide. Col hadn't been the only one to lose his people. "Col, you need to shift. Talk to them."

A moment later the man she'd grown to care so deeply about so quickly—the man she loved—was standing at her side once again.

He was still covered in blood. The gash across his chest was ugly and red and blood seeped slowly from it, leaving red streaks dripping down his stomach.

"We need to get you to a doctor. That's really bad," she squeaked out, forgetting all about the lion shifter guys staring at them.

"I am fine, *shuarra*. The wound is already healing." He slipped an arm around her waist and pulled her tightly to his side. He then turned back to the two men. "I lost my tribe. I want nothing to do with any of you. I hunt the other dragons because they murdered my family."

"Blood for blood. It is honorable," they murmured.

"We will not interfere. But please reconsider joining us," Kann finished.

"No." Col's voice boomed through the clearing.

The two men bowed quickly, then retreated, silently disappearing into the trees from where they'd come.

Naomi turned and faced Col. "Wait, that's it? These

people are from your world. And you want nothing to do with them. You're alone too. I—"

"I have you, Naomi. You are my soul. None of the tribes were cooperative with each other. Our world was made up of many tribes, and we feuded often. Why would it be different here?"

Her mouth dropped in astonishment. "Do you think that was a good thing?"

He shrugged. "It was our way."

"Well, your way is selfish and lonely. You can't just expect to live out here and never interact with anyone." She pulled back, yanking her hand free from his grip.

He was angry and in pain, but did he really mean what he said? Did he want to remain alone? Isolated?

She'd just decided to come out of self-isolation to be with Col. Now he'd banish himself away from the only other people left from his world.

Col closed the gap between them and reached for her hand again. "Why do you push me away, *shuarra?*"

Naomi pulled her hand back and shook her head. "All that matters is your revenge, isn't it?"

"Justice. Not revenge."

She pointed to the mutilated body of Jaha. "That's revenge. Not justice. You made him suffer."

"I was carrying you. Protecting you. I could not be swift." His tone was layered with frustration and fear and an unspoken hint of anger.

"You could've put me down. Hidden me in the trees." She raised her voice.

He could snarl all he wanted, but she didn't fear him. He cared for her too much. Even now, as his anger grew and boiled inside of him, he wasn't advancing on her. Wasn't trying to intimidate her. He was just angry.

Everyone had the right to be angry once in a while. Col was still grieving for the loss of his family. How could he not?

She knew what it was like to grieve. All too well.

"It was not safe!" he roared.

Naomi winced at the sudden outburst.

His eyes went wide, and he backed away as if she'd hit him. An instant later he was a dragon again. Huge and stomping and angry. He moved a safe distance away and took his frustration out on a clump of tall spruce trees. By the time he was finished they were a burning pile of twigs and splinters.

Col backed away from the mess he'd created. His great shoulders physically slumped. His wings drooped. Even his head hung low as if he were ashamed of his behavior.

She trudged across the clearing and put a hand on his chest. "Put out the fire, then we need to go."

He chuffed out a heavy breath but did as she said. He turned his wings on the flames and pumped them until the burning pile of trees and stumps were completely covered by snow. The flames were out. The smoke in the sky faded away into nothing as the wind dispersed it. Then he shifted again.

Col stood silently, staring at the hill of snow and charred sticks. "I acted as a youngling. I frightened you, *shuarra*. I am ashamed."

Naomi sighed and moved to stand next to him. "I forgive you for frightening me."

He didn't turn and meet her gaze. He just kept staring out into the distance.

"You're grieving, Col. Believe me, I know how that feels. You lost your family. Your people. Your home. *All* in a matter of hours. You're angry. Sad and hurt. Anyone would be. But I need you to take me back to my things. I have to tell my family I'm okay. I have to check in with my job. I can't—"

"You would leave me?" he asked softly, finally turning to meet her gaze. His eyes were flickering gold. "You cannot. You are bound to me. You are my soul, *shuarra*. I forbid it." His voice went from disbelief to anger once again.

"I don't want to leave you, you, big barbarian. But I also refuse to let my family think I'm *dead*. I'm more worried about you leaving me. She could kill you. Then where would our souls be. Hmmm? Tell me that." Naomi's tone was flat and tired. The hairs on the back of her neck were standing on end. Her nerves were shot. She'd passed out, puked, met more Reylean shifters, witnessed a dragon temper tantrum, and now he was forbidding her from leaving?

She wasn't even trying to leave!

Aaaaahhhrrrghh!

"I made a vow. Justice will be served." Col's tone darkened, and his eyes narrowed.

"Even if it means you die?" she shot back, struggling to hold in the tears that wanted to spill down her cheeks.

"Trust me, *shuarra*. I will not die."

"Accidents happen. Look at your chest."

He didn't speak. Just shifted without another word, scooped her up and launched himself into the air.

Naomi shrieked and clung to the claws he had carefully wrapped around her body, cradling her against his chest. The cry was more out of surprise than fright.

Asshole.

He could've at least warned her.

They went over several small hills and a cliff before she recognized the landscape. Within a few minutes, they were landing again. This time, they were back in the clearing where her camera bag and snowmachine were parked.

Col let her down gently and shifted back to his human form.

"Just let it go. Let her go. For me. Please." The plea came from her lips as soon as her feet hit the ground. "Let's just move forward together. Create a life here. Vengeance won't bring your family back."

He shook his head. "Blood will have blood. It is our way," he answered.

Naomi shuddered back a sob.

Col reached for her, and she backed up a few quick steps.

"No," she murmured. "Just don't."

He bit off a snarl but didn't argue. He walked to her black camera bag. It stuck out against the snow where she'd dropped it when the dragons had attacked. Col picked it up and then walked with her to the covered snowmachine.

Naomi pulled the blue tarp off, rolled it up, and tied it to the back with a bungie cord. The camera bag would fit right on top. She took it from her dragon and tied it into place too.

There was still room for both of them to ride. She'd packed light, not expecting to be out more than a few hours taking wildlife photos.

"It is not an animal. How will this move you?"

"It's a vehicle. It burns gas to run."

"It has no legs." Confusion hung in his voice like a heavy burden. He continued to stare at the machine.

She swung a leg over and scooted up to the front. "Climb on behind me, and I'll show you."

He gave her another hesitant look.

"Really? I let you carry me in the sky in your claws and you won't trust me enough to climb on a snow-machine?"

With a snort of disgust, he complied. Her dragon threw his leg behind her over the seat and slipped his hands around her waist.

All her nerve endings fired, and her core ached hungrily.

Eternally horny. That's what you get for sleeping with an alien.

She took a deep breath and yanked the cord to start the motor. It growled and chugged but didn't turn over.

Come on. Come on. You can do this.

She yanked again, and the engine roared to life.

Col's arms tightened around her, but he didn't move or say a word.

Naomi used her hand to squeeze the throttle and the snowmachine lurched forward. She leaned to the right and headed for the marked trail only a few dozen yards away. It'd taken her about an hour to come up this far, so going back down should be a little faster.

The noise of the vehicle inhibited conversation, but it was nice to just feel Col behind her. Have his hands wrapped around her. The wind ruffled her curls, even beneath her hood.

Col should've been cold, but nothing seemed to affect him. His chest was like a heater pressed against her back.

Honestly, she was surprised she didn't mind the cold as much as she had when she'd first gotten to Alaska. Maybe she was just adjusting.

Mostly right now, Naomi was just looking forward to a hot shower. Soap. Clean clothes. Then a call to her magazine and to her sister who was probably freaking out since she'd missed her nightly Skype call last evening.

Maybe later, Col would be willing to consider letting the vengeance thing drop. The very thought of what would happen to her if that other dragon had killed him made her ill. He called her his *soul*. He felt like the other half of hers.

CHAPTER
TEN

COL

H is mate was sad. Col could feel it in the tension of her body. She didn't lean into him or desire him. Her arousal had all but disappeared from her sweet scent. He'd fix it once they were inside.

She wouldn't be able to think about anything, but how much he adored and loved her. Naomi was his mate. She was everything.

But, she'd been right to call him angry. And he was grieving.

The death of Jaha had brought some satisfaction in the moment, but it hadn't fixed anything. Nothing he did would bring his family or tribe back. They were lost. He'd vowed to bring his family justice. The only way to satisfy his vow was to take down Sefa too.

Even though he'd upset his *shuarra*, his course would

not alter. That Naomi feared for his life warmed his warrior's heart. Col would beat the female traitor. She stood no chance against his years of training. He'd prove to his mate she had no need to fear.

He squeezed his arms around Naomi's waist a little tighter. She was directing the vehicle toward a cabin just up ahead.

The journey was finished on the strange *snowmachine*. Col still didn't understand how it moved or growled when it wasn't alive. This was a strange world to him. He had a lot to learn.

Naomi was changing too. She had much to learn about what she was becoming.

He hadn't realized the bond would change her, but there'd been too many instances now to ignore. The wound on her head had healed almost immediately after he'd claimed her with his bite. There wasn't even the slightest mark on her smooth sandy skin.

For a Reylean to heal that fast was not uncommon. It hadn't been a bad wound. She'd been shocked. Then today in the fight with Jaha, she'd been exposed to dragon fire. He hadn't been able to shield her. Col had feared he'd failed and lost her. Yet, she wasn't burned.

Just like ... a dragon.

All Reyleans healed quickly, but only the Dragon Tribe were impervious to heat and flame. Naomi wasn't a dragon. Her eyes didn't flicker with gold. She hadn't shifted. She wasn't a dragon, but she was warmer. Her core temperature nearly matched his now.

The changes had been so gradual he'd barely noticed. She stopped the vehicle in front of the steps to the door. The growling stopped, and Col climbed off first, then turned and offered his hand to help her to her feet.

After she'd successfully dismounted the snowmachine, he followed her up the stairs and watched, intrigued as she fiddled with a small black box on the wall. She pressed in some metal tips, and it opened, revealing a small flat gold piece of metal.

"What is it?" he asked.

"A key. To open the door." She grabbed it from the box and moved to the door. She slid the front of the golden *key* into a small crevice on the handle. It clicked and then the door swung open.

The air inside the cabin was cold, but not as biting as outside.

"Oh, I forgot to grab my camera bag."

"I'll get it." Col turned immediately to retrieve his mate's bag. He untied it from the now quiet machine and returned quickly to the cabin.

This shelter appeared a bit larger than the one they'd spent the last few days inside. Where was the bed?

He laid the bag on the couch and wandered to the back, through a dark hallway. The first door he opened was the washroom, with a sink and shower just like the previous cabin. This one also had a large tank in the corner filled with water.

Col closed it and continued to the next door. It opened to reveal a room for sleep. Naomi's scent filled the room. A few pieces of her clothing were hanging over a chair in the corner of the room.

The bed was large and higher than the one at the other cabin. Both were so different than the furs and skins he was used to sleeping on at home. His people moved constantly, but it seemed his mate was used to more permanent living quarters.

These wooden shelters were not mobile, like the tents his family and tribe lived in. This world was harsher, and the cold did bite at the skin after a while. Stronger shelters were probably necessary.

He returned to the center of the cabin to find Naomi cutting up some type of orange food.

"I needed something to eat. Want a piece of carrot?"

Col shook his head. Then walked up to her, took the knife and pulled her out of the kitchen.

"Hey." She yanked her hand back. "I'm hungry. And we need to talk more about that other dragon."

"We can talk later." He wrapped an arm around her waist.

"No, I feel disgusting. We're not having sex. I need to eat. I need to shower."

He redirected his path. "I will wash you then."

"Why do I feel like that's going to turn into sex too?" Naomi gave him a wary look but allowed him to continue pulling her all the way into the washroom.

"Executing Sefa is something I must do. I must deliver justice to my family. It would be dishonorable to allow her crime to stand unpunished." He released her for a moment to turn on the water in the shower. She'd taught him how to use this indoor plumbing as she had back at the hunter's cabin. These knobs looked slightly different, but the markings were the same. Soon the large stone and glass shower stall was filled with steam and waiting for them.

"What if she kills you?"

"You will not lose me, *shuarra*." Col's tone deepened to that silky darkness that made her body turn to mush. "I. Will. Not. Leave. You." His voice dropped even further and took on a commanding quality. "Say it."

"You will—"

"You are my heart and soul, Naomi, but you cannot ask me to fail my family. Say it," he asked again, waiting to hear her repeat his words of assurance. "I must hear that you believe in me. That you trust me to take care of you."

"You will not leave me?" She couldn't lose him.

"I will not." His dragon rumbled softly in his chest.

"I trust you."

"Good."

"You're purring again." The sound relaxed the tension from her body as if the vibrations were running through each and every one of her muscles.

"My dragon is pleased that you trust me," he answered simply, tugging at the zipper on her coat.

She let him undo it and toss the puffy coat to the ground.

"Naomi, I have trained for nearly two decades as a warrior. Jaha was a warrior as well, but not as skilled or as tested. His sister has no experience. She has never fought or trained a day in her life. She is a coward and traitor and a murderer."

His mate nodded slowly.

"But when I fight her, you must stay behind. I will not risk you again."

"Again?" Her voice trembled.

"During the fight with Jaha." Each word he spoke was slow and defined. "I failed to protect you from one attack. I'd thought for sure I clutched no more than your burned corpse. But when I landed and set you down on the snow … it was as if nothing had touched you. Not a single hair had been singed. Not even your clothes." He tugged the hem of her shirt.

She lifted her arms and let him pull it over her head, baring most of her skin. Except for her breasts. Those were secured in a piece of clothing she'd said was called a bra.

He kissed her shoulders, shoving at the straps in his way.

She unhooked it and let the bra drop to the ground.

"You survived dragon fire."

"I w-what?" Naomi choked out. "How's that possible?"

"Our tribe is blessed with a certain type of magick. Our skin is impervious to heat and flame. Whatever is touching our body takes on those properties."

"Like you sweat fire retardant or something?" she asked, with a hint of disbelief in her voice. "Then I wasn't burned, because we'd been having sex. I was covered in your sweat. And you were holding me against your dragon's body. Maybe your dragon sweats the stuff too."

"Perhaps." He stroked the soft skin of her bare shoulder. "But I think you are changing. Your wound healed very quickly."

"What? You think I'm becoming Reylean? I think the flame-retardant sweat thing is way more likely." She chuckled and shook her head. "Just because I healed, doesn't mean I'm changing. Maybe the cut wasn't really that bad."

Col smiled but didn't speak again.

Was it possible?

He'd never heard of a dragon being able to protect someone completely before. There were no stories. Nothing. Dragons didn't burn. Or was there another explanation.

Her wound had healed quickly. Her raised core temperature. The fever after his bite. Had her body changed? Become more like a dragon?

Even the lions had said she scented as Dragon Tribe. It wasn't just his scent. There *was* something different.

His dragon purred in his chest again, knocking him loose from his thoughts. He looked down and smiled, pleased by the sight of his nearly naked mate.

Col lipped and nipped and kissed his way down Naomi's shoulder blades until he found her hard pebbled nipples. So beautiful. So perfect. He'd feast upon her and make her forget all the things that troubled her mind.

At least for a while.

CHAPTER
ELEVEN

NAOMI

N aomi gasped as Col lavished attention on her breasts. Licking. Sucking. Nipping. Her core was throbbing in moments. Her objections and worries were melting away like the snow in a spring thaw.

That'd been his plan all along ... and it was working.

His hands trailed to her waist. He was undoing her jeans now and pulling them down her legs. Then her pants were gone, and he was leading her into the hot shower stall.

The water was scalding, but it felt so good. She stepped into the center of the water stream and let it sluice comfortingly over her body.

All she could feel was the soothing presence of the water and Col's hands working soap up and down the length of her body. Her mind left her worries and focused on *him*.

On the here and now.

She grabbed the bar of soap from her dragon man and worked up a lather on his hard muscles as well, being sure to cover every single inch. Water flowed over them as they moved, washing away the dirt and the blood and the worry.

Naomi got some shampoo and worked it into his shoulder-length brown hair. He was so gorgeous. Her own personal barbarian warrior. He was cut like a superhero. Hard abs that led down in a V-line to a more than impressive cock. Arms like freaking granite. Nothing about him was soft, except the way he cared for her.

He returned the favor, massaging shampoo into her curls. Rubbing until everything just drifted away on the steam of the shower. The water was scalding; hotter than she would've normally had it before. Now it felt so good. Almost like she was bathing in fire.

Was there any merit to what he'd said? Was she really changing? Was that possible?

Once the shampoo was rinsed away, she turned in the shower, pressing her aching breasts against his chest.

Col didn't need any more encouragement. His cock was hard and insistently nudging her stomach. "Naomi." His voice was a deep growl that turned every brain cell to mush.

Anything he wanted. Everything he wanted.

"Yes," she murmured.

His hands skimmed over her back from her waist up to her shoulders, then down to cup her breasts. He thumbed the hardened nipples and she hissed out a quick breath. If he wasn't careful, she was liable to come right then. Just from that.

Col turned her, so his back was to the water, then knelt down, grabbed one of her calves and lifted it to rest over his shoulder.

Naomi gasped for air as he kissed the inside of her leg, starting at her knee and running up the back of her thigh. She stared down as he drew nearer to her throbbing, aching, and needy core.

He pushed her back until her ass hit the tile wall. At least now she wouldn't fall on him once her legs started to shake. His tongue swirled over her clit and all rational thought exited her mind. There was only him. All she could feel was his hands on her body. His mouth on her sex. All she wanted to feel was him.

"Please," she murmured, moaning through the onslaught of pleasure.

He sucked harder and she bit her lip to keep from screaming.

"Don't hold it in, *shuarra*. Cry out for me. I want to hear your pleasure." Col's voice came out husky and dark. A rumble vibrated through his chest and echoed in the steam-filled shower stall.

"Col, I need more." She flexed her hips to angle her sex even closer to his mouth.

"Fly for me, Naomi." He sucked again, slowly, but harder. Then he slipped two fingers inside, rubbing and stretching until the ache of need throbbed through her entire body.

She shuddered. The climax was so close. Her chest tightened, and she sucked in a desperate breath.

He reached up with his free hand to tweak one of her hard-as-a-rock nipples.

Naomi joined in, playing with the other.

Then he curled the fingers of his other hand inside her as his tongue drew circles on her flesh.

Closer. More.

Col pushed her harder into the wall and slid his fingers deeper.

She careened over the edge, screaming as her body imploded. The orgasm rocked through her like an avalanche, rolling and tumbling and crashing down. No escape. Her breasts ached under his hand.

Naomi floated high, and her legs trembled and gave out, but Col was ready.

He caught her weight and let her slowly slide down to the water-heated tile on the floor next to him. His mouth trailed along her skin, from her stomach up to her breasts. Latched onto a nipple, and she whimpered at the overwhelming sensations flooding through her system.

No more. She couldn't take more. She shoved his head away, and he grinned at her with a sexy smile that made her core ache and miss his mouth already.

She couldn't get enough of him. Ever.

"*Shuarra.*" His tone sung of his need for her. He stood, lifting her as he went.

"Yes," she moaned. She needed him too. So much.

He hooked one of her legs over his arm and pushed her against the wall again. His cock nudged her entrance for a second before sliding home.

"Yes," she cried out again, her voice as husky and as dark as his.

Col stroked inside, and she clamped down on him hard. He groaned, burying his mouth in her neck.

She clutched at his slick arms. His back, dragging her nails down his body in a desperate attempt to pull him closer. The water from the shower pounded his back and made it slick. "Col, yes." She synced her hips with his thrusts. Then hopped up just a little on one foot, trying to get higher and hoping he'd get the idea.

He did. Col's hands moved to cup her ass, lifting her off the ground.

Naomi hooked her heels behind him, and he thrust harder. They moved in unison with each drive, gasping together.

He looked into her eyes and kissed her, locked in an embrace she never wanted to end.

A cry erupted from her throat. Another orgasm crashed through her, and Col came right along for the ride. She tightened around him, and her fingers dug into his flesh. Everything swirled and careened.

She came hard and fast, and he roared, shaking the glass door on the shower stall as he spilled into her, thrusting and shoving her into the wall hard enough to knock the breath from her lungs.

Amazing.

She gasped for a breath as he held her frozen in place.

His cock throbbing and still buried deeply inside her. He'd come, but it felt as though he could go another round or two without a second thought.

"My *shuarra,* you please me so much," Col rumbled, nipping at her ear before pulling away. His hands encircled her waist and with one fluid movement he withdrew and turned her away from him. He put a hand flat on the middle of her back and pushed gently until she was flat against the tile wall, belly to stone.

He wasn't done.

Her core lit with excitement and anticipation. Naomi sucked in a deep breath, but nothing could prepare her for the ferocity of him taking her again so quickly.

He grabbed her ass, pushed her up and sank into her with a quick groan.

Another cry escaped her throat. Col was so hard and hitting so deep from behind her. Her arousal ratcheted up and soared, building toward yet another climax.

This dragon man, the way he touched her, it was indescribable. Amazing.

"Col!" The next orgasm overtook her with his very next thrust, ripping through her core and radiating out from her center like a nuclear wave, growing wider and wider.

He snarled and drove deep one more time before joining her on the path to ecstasy.

SHE WOKE LATER in bed with her body nestled against Col's. How much later was difficult to determine. The sun was still shining brightly outside through the curtains in the bedroom. Her dragon man was on his back, and she had her head in the crook of his shoulder, with one arm and one leg thrown over his wide body. The blankets covered them, and she was so warm. Everything smelled like Col, like fire and spice and man.

As much as she didn't want to leave the comfort of her mate's arms, she had to call her family and let them know she hadn't died out in the Alaskan wilderness. Naomi also needed to download the photos from her shoot and send them to her magazine. They were already going to be pissed that she didn't check in yesterday.

She extracted herself carefully from Col's arms, then the bed. She pulled on a pair of yoga pants and a sweatshirt from her suitcase in the corner and padded quietly out of the bedroom.

Naomi filled a glass of water from the tank in the kitchen next to the sink before making her way over to the small desk in the corner of the living room where her laptop awaited.

She pulled the memory card from the camera and plugged it into her adapter. The pictures popped up on the screen. Elk. Birds. A fox. That had been a lucky catch. Dragon.

Holy shit.

She had taken a picture of Jaha and his sister right before they'd come at her. Naomi clicked again.

Another picture of the two dragons.

DELETE.

She selected the pictures as fast as her computer would let her. Couldn't keep something like that in her cloud. If anyone ever saw it, Col would be in danger.

The picture zapped to the trash can, and she emptied it immediately. Hopefully it'd been fast enough. Privacy was a joke. The government had bots that looked at everything online. That one hadn't uploaded yet though, she'd deleted it before it went into the cloud. It wasn't on the memory card anymore.

Gone.

It was gone.

Naomi took a deep breath and let it shudder from her lungs slowly. She hadn't even remembered taking the pictures. When Jaha had hurt her, it'd knocked even the surrounding memories around that time into the dark.

Col said the black dragon had thrown her across the clearing. She'd hit a tree, which'd been why her head throbbed after she woke up in that cabin like an elephant had stepped on her. But her man was right, her head had healed fast. The cut was gone the next day and she never remembered it aching past that next morning either.

Was she really changing? If so, what was happening to her?

Not that having flame retardant skin was a bad thing. Naomi couldn't really see a downside. Really, it was kinda like having a superpower.

She looked down at her hands. No fingerless gloves. She'd been wearing them ever since she got to Alaska. Hadn't been able to bear to take them off. Or socks. She wiggled her toes. No socks either. She wasn't cold. Actually, she felt comfortable.

Naomi swiveled the chair. No fire in the wood stove. They hadn't started one yet. The air in the cabin wasn't particularly warm either, she could feel the chill on the air ... but she was *warm*.

Maybe it was nothing. Maybe she was just warm because she'd been in bed with Col, and he was like sleeping with an electric blanket. Residual warmth. That was all it was. Nothing was changing. She was still human.

She put the memory card back into her camera and packed it back into her bag. Then returned to her laptop and opened her email. The screen loaded.

Naomi went to her work account first and cringed. Five emails from her boss.

Dammit.

She hit reply on the last one and tried to apologize and explain that she'd had an accident and had been out of reach for the last twenty-four hours or so. She uploaded the link to her storage drive with the photos and sent a quick email that said she'd be in touch soon.

Would like to tell him she'd be quitting...

Naomi might have issues with Col going off to kill the bad dragon, but she had no intention of leaving Alaska. Asking him to come to New York would be like asking a T-Rex to live in Central Park. Not happening.

Alaska was beautiful. She could get used to it as long as she had Col. She'd have to lie to more people than just her boss. Wouldn't be able to tell anyone about her dragon man. Ever. Not even her family. They'd just have to think she met some logger while she was on her business trip and fell head over heels. They'd be sad she was moving, but they'd probably be thrilled that she was moving on.

She plugged in her earbuds and opened the Skype app. Then dialed her sister.

Naomi didn't know what time it was back in New York

—maybe early evening—but Camila would have her phone next to her no matter what. Especially if she was waiting for her to call. Since she was supposed to call every single night and hadn't last night, her sister would be pissed. Not that her family was controlling. They were just super close.

She and Camila talked every day. In fact, Naomi couldn't remember the last time she'd missed their nightly phone call. They spent almost every weekend together as well. Between shopping and hanging out and Sunday night dinners with the family. It was like she'd never moved out.

"Ohmygod! Nai! *Finally*." Her sister's voice screamed through the app. A moment later her face appeared in the camera window. "You realize you've given me a heart attack. And Mom. What happened to you? We were so scared you'd been eaten by a bear."

Not a bear.

Naomi chuckled inwardly.

Crap.

She needed to call her mother too. Her parents were probably just as worried as Camila, because her sister had likely shared that she hadn't been calling in. "I'm okay, Cam, just had a little accident and—"

"Are you okay?" Her sister's picture went black for a second. "Hang on, I'm adding Mama."

"What! No!" she started. She wasn't ready for the onslaught just yet. Hell, she hadn't even figured out what she was going to tell them yet.

Too late. Her mother's face appeared split on her screen along with Camila's.

"Naomi Maria Parker!" Her mother looked so tired. Red rimmed her eyes like she'd been crying. There were dark circles under them.

All her fault.

"Mama, I'm okay. Just a little accident. I hurt my head and was out of it for a while. I couldn't get to my laptop or phone, but I'm doing better now. I'm so sorry you were worried."

"What happened?" Cam asked from the other screen.

"Snowmachine accident." The words were literally falling from her mouth without permission.

Oh, well. It was as good an excuse as any.

"I hit my head really bad. A local found me and helped me get back to my cabin."

"You're sure nothing is wrong?" her mom asked again.

"I'm fine. Promise."

"Why didn't he take you to a hospital?" Cam asked.

"Probably because the closest one is hundreds of miles from here and you have to fly." Naomi held in a laugh. Technically, Col could've flown her. Not that he would've known where the hospital was. Plus, he would've been a dragon. That wouldn't have gone over well with the locals.

"Holy Toledo! Is that the local?" Camila screeched pointing at the screen. "No wonder you didn't call yesterday."

"Cam." Naomi forced her gaze to the square on the screen where her camera view showed her.

Oh geeze.

Col was standing behind her with a curious expression. By some miracle he was wearing his kilt thing.

So at least he wasn't flashing her mother and her sister. That would've certainly made an impression.

Her sister's mouth twisted into a mischievous grin. "So, did he help you get over the injury personally?"

"Cam," Naomi whined. "That's a personal question, and I'm not—"

"Fine, fine. Whatever. I'll call you back later without Mom on the line, so you can dish," her sister said. "Go be with your local. Call me back later, okay?"

She sighed.

"Aren't you going to introduce me, Naomi? I should at least get to thank the man that saved my daughter's life. Whether or not you decided to reward your savior is none of my business. You're a single woman." Her mother was pointing at the screen now too.

Pointing at Col.

She turned to her mate. "Come on over here, Col. My mother wants to say hi."

He smiled and moved to kneel next to her chair in front of the desk. His head and bare shoulders still showed in the camera view, but at least he wasn't showing off his entire torso anymore.

"What magick is this?" he asked her softly.

"I told you. It's science. This is a phone call." She covered the mic with her hand, so her family couldn't hear. "This world has a lot of technology. It might look like magick. But it's not."

He nodded, but his expression remained doubtful.

Naomi popped out one of her earbuds and put it into his ear, then leaned closer so they could share the mic.

"Col, this is my Mama." She pointed at the picture of her smiling mother. "And this is my sister, Camila." She indicated at the other box on the screen. Camila waved too.

"It's nice to meet you, Col," her mom said. "Thank you for saving my baby girl and taking good care of her."

"Yeah, I bet he took good care of her." Her sister snorted through a laugh.

"Cam," Naomi groaned.

"It is a pleasure to meet family of my *shuarra*." Col's voice was low and even.

"Shoo-ar-ah?" her mother repeated.

"It's just what he calls me. It's Native."

"Um, he said *my*," Camila said. "Girl, you didn't like participate in some tribal marriage ceremony? Are you married?"

"Of course not," she shot back.

Her dragon man opened his mouth, and she could feel the protest coming.

At least he hadn't called her his *mate*. Yet. She put her hand over his mouth and glared, hopefully giving him a look that communicated she wanted him to stop talking.

"Look, I'll call you back later okay. I just wanted to let you guys know I was okay. This was the first time I was back where there was WiFi."

"Naomi, I want—" her mother continued.

"Sorry, Mama." Naomi slapped the laptop closed, ending the call.

Shit. Shit. Shit.

"I thought you were sleeping." Naomi tugged the earbud from Col's ear.

He turned the chair and met her gaze. His eyes flickered gold. "I was sleeping. Then I heard you speaking. I thought someone had come into the cabin. Why were you ashamed when I called you *shuarra*?"

"It wasn't that ... it just ... I don't know how to explain *us* to my family yet," she admitted, wishing she could shrink away or become invisible.

"We are soul mates. You are mine. I am yours. What else is there to say?"

"Well, it sounds so simple when you put it that way. Still, people don't really do that on earth. We don't have magick and soul mates."

"You do now." Col grasped her chin between his fingers.

Naomi's heart fluttered, and a shiver of anticipation made her body throb. Just a small touch made her burn for him.

Made her whole body *need* him.

"Abso-fucking-lutely."

He smiled, obviously pleased with her enthusiastic response. "I can smell your arousal, *shuarra*. Let me satisfy your desire." Her dragon man pushed between her legs and pulled her closer, rolling the chair forward until her crotch was against his chest.

She put a hand against one of his rock-hard pecs and shoved back. "We are not having sex again right now. No more distracting me. I know that's what you were doing in the shower. We—I—I need to know how this is going to work. Where do we even start? I'm not really into living in caves or the wilderness you know."

"Is this not your home?" he asked, gesturing to the room.

Naomi shook her head. "I'm just renting it. I don't live here, Col. I'm new here, just like you. I live in a huge city with millions of people over four thousand miles away from here. We can't stay here either."

CHAPTER
TWELVE

COL

No home. No wonder his mate was unsettled. This cabin was also not hers. She'd only gotten permission to stay a short time.

"I will build you a home, Naomi." He rose from the floor and offered his hand. "Come sit."

She rose from her chair and followed him over to the couch.

He pulled her down across his lap, wrapped a blanket around her—his mate liked blankets—then held her tightly with his arms. Col nuzzled the side of her head and sniffed the lovely perfume of her hair. The soaps she used were soft and blended with her natural scent. Her curls tickled his face, and he rubbed his cheek against them again. So soft. So beautiful was his *shuarra.*

"How?"

"I am strong. I will take care of you. As a dragon or

human." He repeated the word she'd used to describe her people. "I was a prince in my tribe."

"Ah, is that what those guys meant when they called you Heir to the Dragon Lord?"

"Yes, and you will lack for nothing you need. I will learn how to thrive on this world. And I would be honored if you would teach me your people's ways."

"But, I don't know how to live in Alaska. I don't hunt or fish or know how to chop down trees. None of that survival stuff."

Col smiled and buried his nose in his mate's hair again. "I can do all those things, *shuarra*. It is the phones and technology you've spoken of I do not understand. I do not understand how the light in this home works or how you have water flowing from pulling a lever in the washroom. But I can learn. These are all things I can learn."

A shuffling sound outside put him on alert. He couldn't smell through the thick cabin walls. It wasn't like a tent that allowed breezes through. In here he was separated from what was going on outside.

"What is it?" Naomi asked, tensing in his lap.

"Someone is outside," he murmured. He slid out from under her on the couch and walked to the side of the door.

The window was covered by draping fabric. If he pulled it away, whoever was outside would know he'd heard them. He glanced around the room and into the kitchen. There was another door in the back.

"Stay here."

"What? Wait. Where are you going?"

Col pointed at the kitchen door.

"Why don't we just open the door and see who it is? It could be the landlord for the cabin checking up on me." A brusque knock on the door followed her statement. "See." She pointed. "Would the evil dragon knock?"

He curled his lip in irritation, but he agreed with her. Sefa would not knock. In fact, if Jaha's sister had tracked them here, it was much more likely that she would land on the roof and rip it off to get at them. Col chose not to share that scenario with Naomi.

His mate moved across the room, blanket still wrapped around her, to open the door.

"Naomi." He called her back, but it was too late, the door was already opening. He charged forward, pushing her behind him as he met the golden flicker of a gaze standing in front of him.

The man pushed back a furry hood and gave a slight bow of his head. "Col of House of Li'Vhram, Heir of the Dragon Lord. I am Tor. Kann and Saul said—"

"You are Tiger Tribe. Why are you here? Did you track us?"

"We did," the large redheaded man said stepping down a stair. "The dragon left alive on the mountain is vicious. She has killed several wolves already. The three of us had no desire to be her next target." He gestured behind him.

Col saw the two familiar lion shifter males standing back a few yards. "What do you want?"

"Kann said you have a human mate," he replied. "We have spent nights in the forest. One night in an abandoned shelter before humans came. We left before they saw us. This world is strange. We don't know how to approach people. We tried at one home to ask for a meal and they shot a weapon at us and told us not to come around again. We have been hesitant to hunt as our animals as there are many human hunters nearby."

A soft hand touched his arm and tugged. "Col, let them in."

"No." He faced his mate.

She dropped the blanket to the floor, crossed her arms over her chest and gave him a hard glare.

It was similar to the look that his mother would give when he and his sister had misbehaved.

"I am not a youngling. That will not work on me."

"These men are almost all that's left of your entire world, and you would turn them away?"

"*Shuarra*." He bared his teeth, let his fangs descend, hoping she would back down.

She did not.

"I know better." Naomi flashed a smile he wasn't going to be able to intimidate her. Not that he truly wanted to do so. "Your dragon would die before it hurt me. It's probably angry at you just for growling."

His dragon rumbled its agreement.

Col snorted in disgust. "It is not safe." He turned back to the tiger shifter who'd stepped down off the stairs to wait for an answer.

Neither he nor the other two males showed signs of stress or fear. Their hearts beat steadily. Their faces held nothing more than quiet hope.

If he'd come through the portal alone and hadn't found Naomi, would he be in the same predicament?

He was a dragon. He probably would've just lived up at the top of the mountain, eating what he could catch.

But he wasn't alone. He had Naomi.

"You have to trust some people Col. Not all of them will let you down."

"You were my mate. I knew I could trust you."

"Let them in. I have enough food to at least give you all one good meal. Then we figure out what to do from there." Naomi stepped closer and looked outside.

The cold bitter wind rushed past her, blowing her curls around her head. Beautiful. Wild. Free.

She had such a kind heart. After everything she'd been through with her past, and then with him, she was still willing to extend hospitality to even more strangers.

"Very well." He turned to the doorway again, disapproving of Naomi's choice, but willing to make the effort on her behalf. "You may come in. Should you attempt to hurt my mate, I will kill you by roasting your flesh slowly while you remain alive."

Tor visibly gulped and bowed his head again, soothing Col's need to see that they feared him.

The other two—the lions—approached, and he moved away from the doorway to allow them inside.

Col pushed Naomi behind him again, still waiting for their pretense to fall and a fight to start. Decades of unrest didn't just vanish over the course of a few days.

No one moved angrily. All three trooped in wearing heavy fur coats and their traditional warrior kilt garb and soft leather boots. Just like his, except designed with their tribal colors. The Dragon Tribe wore purple. He had no need for the coat, but not all Reyleans burned as warm as dragons.

"I'm Naomi." His mate pushed his arm aside and took a step forward toward Tor. She held out her hand as if offering it to the tiger to touch.

His dragon roared inside, and he snarled. He caught her around the waist and hauled her back against him. "No one touches you, *shuarra*."

The males stood silent and wide-eyed. Probably waiting for his dragon to shift, destroy the cabin, and kill them all.

Col was tempted.

"I was just offering my hand. It's what humans do to say hello!" Naomi screeched. "Put me down. I swear if this was *Star Trek*, you'd all be a bunch of Klingons. Hot Klingons, but still. Klingons. Minus the bumps on the face of course."

He set her down over beside the desk and her *laptop*. Her words didn't mean anything to him. No frame of reference for this thing called a *Klingon*.

But she was frustrated. That he could easily tell by her tone of voice.

"No touching as a greeting." Col pinned her with his gaze. "It is not our way. You are mine. I am not only Reylean, I am the son of a royal House. It would be a grave dishonor for them to touch my mate. They should bow."

The fight went out of her body, and she peered around his shoulder at the three silent men standing in the middle of the living room. All of them had bent at the waist in a deep bow. "I didn't mean to dishonor you or put them in a bad way." Naomi's voice calmed. "We don't have the same customs. How was I supposed to know?"

He paused. His dragon still vibrated in his chest, a low rumbling growl warning all how close it was to bursting out.

She was correct. She wouldn't have any knowledge of his world's customs, just as he had no knowledge of hers. Also, why the other men were likely having trouble making their way with other humans. Because they did not know the expectations of this world.

All three men released a slow sigh and stood straight and silent, as if waiting for instruction.

Col sighed. "Sit." He gestured to the small table and four chairs near the cooking space. "Naomi," he gestured to the last chair.

She moved quickly, grabbing her blanket off the floor and wrapping it around her shoulders again. "What about you?" She slid into the chair and looked over her shoulder and up at him.

"I will stand behind you, *shuarra*."

She turned back to the group and frowned. "I'm guessing hugs aren't really a thing with your people either, huh?"

The tiger spoke up. "What is a hug?"

"An embrace. Humans hug each other when they feel strong emotion or a strong connection to someone," Naomi continued.

Kann shook his head. "Mates embrace. Parents embrace their children." The others nodded their heads in agreement.

"Males in the same tribe will clasp wrists in a

welcoming gesture," Tor said. "Is that what you were trying to do earlier?"

His mate sighed. "Kinda. Not really though." She turned and took Col's hand, then shook it up and down. He watched her carefully. "That's a handshake. It's pretty common in human culture." She stood and took a step away from him. "Especially for introducing yourself. You hold out your hand and wait. If the other person is friendly. They take it." Naomi gestured for him to take her hand again in demonstration.

He did, curling his fingers around hers gently.

She shook his hand again, not hard, but firmly. "Then you introduce yourself. Like, hello, my name is Naomi Parker."

"Parker, is that your House or tribe?" Kann asked.

"It's called a family name here."

They all listened intently to his mate.

As much as he hated them being here, interrupting his time with his mate, they were smart to have returned to seek wisdom.

"What if the human is not friendly?" Tor asked.

"They won't take your hand." His mate frowned, and her expression turned thoughtful. "Either they are just unfriendly, or they see you as a threat. Some might even pull a gun on you."

"What is a gun?"

"It's a human weapon. They come in all sizes, but they are all metal and they shoot bullets through the air that will tear a hole right through your body. Most you'll see up here are hunting rifles."

The men nodded. "We have already encountered these weapons."

"I'm not surprised. You guys seriously look like you stepped out of a *Lord of the Rings* movie or *Game of Thrones*. You could certainly give the northern wildlings a run for their money. They probably thought you were crazy, or they were just scared of you."

Col pulled her to his side and nuzzled her hair, breathing in her scent.

Naomi didn't pull away, she just leaned against him and let him fondle her curls. As if she knew he needed her to calm himself.

"I am Tor." The tiger shifter gestured to himself. "Saul and Kann came through the portal right behind me. We all ended up at the same cave looking for shelter."

"Others?" Col asked.

"I scented a couple from the Bear Tribe. We scented Wolf Tribe too. So, there are others. Not sure how many. When the volcano on Reylea began to breathe fire right below the portal, it was too late for most of us. The ground began to fall out from under our feet. Great chunks of burning rocks fell from the sky. A few of us managed to scramble through right before the magick-bender was killed. The portal closed after that."

So many dead. So many had lost their entire family. Their whole tribe.

Naomi squeezed his hand, as if sensing the wave of pain that swept through him.

His whole world had perished. Not just his family and tribe, but nearly every person in the entire N'ra Lowlands.

"There were rumors of other magick-benders. Other portals across the mountains, but I don't know how any of our people could've gotten out of the lowlands in time." Saul's tone was tired and worn. "Burning rivers of fire were engulfing everything when I leapt through the horizon."

The other nodded in agreement.

Col stayed silent. He'd entered the portal hours before anyone else. No one had even made it to the top of the mountain yet.

A twinge of guilt weighed on his heart. How many people could he have saved if he hadn't chased after Sefa and Jaha?

He'd abandoned his world to seek justice, but at what price?

Would seeking out Sefa cost him more?

He was pulled from his thoughts when Naomi stepped away from his side.

"You sit, Col. Let me make some food. I know I have enough for spaghetti. Not sure what else is left."

"I could hunt something for you, *shuarra*."

She shook her head. "The fireplace isn't big enough to roast anything in. It would be a waste of an animal. I don't have any way to cook it, and I'm not about to watch all of you turn and eat something raw." His mate made a hacking noise in her throat and swallowed loudly. "I have some sausage and pasta and sauce. It won't be a lot, but it will hold us until we head back to McKinley Park. I can probably get the owner of this cabin to rent it to me a bit longer. But it's not big enough for all of us to stay together."

"They will not sleep here." Col's tone was short and final.

"Very well, then we'll need to see about getting a place for them to stay. Maybe there's someone with a hunting cabin who will let them stay cheap."

"Cheap?" Tor asked.

"I'm assuming none of you have any money," she answered. "I paid to stay here. I bought the food. You need money to live in this world. Everyone works."

"We don't need much," Saul said. "We can build a shelter. Live off the game of the land."

"Okay, well. How are you going to buy the land?" Naomi asked.

The other men fell silent.

Col stared at his mate. Of course, the people here would've already divided the land among themselves. They were newcomers in a territory. In Reylea, wars were fought over land, but here land was apparently acquired with wealth.

"I've got some savings, but it won't be enough for very long unless we figure out a way to barter."

"You are very knowledgeable, Naomi. Thank you for agreeing to help us. And thank you Col of House Li'Vhram for your hospitality." Tor stood from his chair. "If I could find you some small animals, Naomi, would that be a good addition to your speh-geeh-tee?"

His mate nodded and then made a strange face. "I don't know how to peel anything or take the guts out." She wrung her hands in front of her. "My grandparents lived in a little town north of New York. We ate rabbits and other varmints, but I never learned about hunting or cleaning stuff."

Tor smiled and bowed his head respectfully. "I shall prepare everything for you." He met Col's gaze for a moment. Bowed again then left the cabin.

He turned back to the table.

The two lion shifters were sitting quietly, looking nervous.

Naomi had moved to the cooking area and was putting a pot onto the thing she called a *stovetop*. It warmed like a fake fire to heat the pots.

This was really moving forward. Three tribes were going to work together. His father would be shocked, but this was the right path. Even if Col didn't stay close to these men, they needed his *shuarra's* help to survive in this world.

They all did.

Including himself.

CHAPTER
THIRTEEN

NAOMI

Naomi filled the pot with a few cups of water from the small blue water tank sitting on the counter next to the sink. There was running water in the bathroom, thanks to the storage tank and heater, but the cabin was still technically dry. The hole in the kitchen sink drained to a gray water bucket in the cabinet beneath.

She put the large pot on the stove to boil and turned to peer out the window to her left. Snow was falling hard now, blowing almost sideways. The skies were filled with dark clouds, blocking out the daylight. It was only noon. The land and the sky nearly blended together now. She couldn't see more than maybe a hundred feet from the cabin.

The wind rattled the shutters and a loud ring from the wall behind her nearly made her jump out of her skin.

All three men leapt up, knocking their chairs to the floor in the process.

Col rushed to her side a growl tearing from his throat. "What magick is this?"

"Hey, it's just the phone. Remember you talked to my mom and sister on the phone."

"That was on your *laptop*." He glanced at her computer on the desk.

"Yep, and this is the phone." Naomi pointed to the old school tan plastic phone hanging on the wall. She pushed his hands off her waist and picked up the receiver. The cord dangled nearly to the floor. She smiled and shook her head, hadn't used one of these since the last trip to Grandma's house. "Hello?"

"Oh, Ms. Parker. I called yesterday hoping to catch you."

"Sorry, I got stuck up on a mountain. But I'm back. And actually, I was going to call you and see if it would be possible to keep the cabin longer. Maybe another week?"

"Oh, sure. Nobody rents this far out from the resort during the winter season. You're welcome to stay. I don't have any reservations on the books for several months. But, I wanted to warn you. There's a storm coming in right now. You shouldn't leave the cabin until the snow lets up, and if you need help digging out the snowmachine, just call me. I'll come or send my son to help you."

Col growled next to her. He had his ear next to the phone listening.

"Thank you, Mr. Curtis. Do you know how long the storm is supposed to last?"

"Supposed to blow out late tonight, is what they're saying."

"Thank you. I'll call if I need anything."

"Yes, ma'am. There should be plenty of wood stacked outside the kitchen door for the wood stove, and the tank should have enough water for another week or so if you're careful."

"Thank you again, Mr. Curtis." Naomi hung the receiver back onto the wall base.

"You need nothing from this Misss-ster Kerr-tass." Col straightened to his full height and puffed out his chest. So big and protective. Totally different than her brothers getting up in her business.

"No, I don't. But I also don't want him to know the four of you are up here either. At least not yet."

Her dragon man grunted and walked back toward the table, leaving her in the kitchen.

She held in a chuckle and returned to opening the two jars of sauce she'd brought up with her. There wasn't much left in the fridge. A side of bacon. A dozen eggs. Naomi had a couple loaves of bread on the counter next to the toaster. A box of wine. She was definitely breaking that out after the meal.

"Col, would you start a fire in the wood stove." She pointed to the black cast iron giant in the corner of the living room.

He rose reluctantly from the table, giving the other men a warning look.

She wasn't sure what he thought they'd do, but then again, she didn't know his world like he did. She had to keep reminding herself that these men—shifters—weren't from this world.

They had different customs and beliefs and traditions, and they were primitive. No plumbing. No electricity. From what she'd gleaned so far from Col, they lived mainly in tents and had always been nomadic. At least his tribe had.

She leaned against the counter and caught one of the other shifter's attention. "Are you all nomadic?"

Saul, the one with the loose blond hair and feathers in his braids, cast a quick glance at Col before answering. "Not all the tribes. The dragons were the most nomadic. They would move from valley to valley. The Lion Tribe lived similarly though. We moved with the herds of game on the plains. We did not live in places like this," he gestured to the room. "Like the dragon tribe we would live in large tents. Usually, each family would have a communal room for gathering and cooking and eating. Then separate spaces for sleeping."

"Tiger Tribe and Panther Tribe, from the jungles lived in more permanent homes. Usually high in the trees to avoid the annual floods." Col stood and moved back to the kitchen.

"I guess Tor is really missing his warm jungle, huh?" Naomi asked, giving Col a smile. "Thank you for getting the fire started in the stove. The air was getting a little cold, even for me."

He returned to her side and pulled her against his body. He was so warm. Seriously, his skin felt like an electric heating pad. Not a bad thing in this kind of climate.

She wrapped her hands around his waist and hugged

him tight, snuggling her face against the bare skin of his chest. Unlike the other shifters who had scruff or short beards, Col had no facial hair or body hair.

Just long wavy brown locks that draped down his shoulders, longer than she'd ever grown out her crazy curls. Naomi didn't have anything against beards, but she was glad Col didn't have one.

Saul chuckled. "Except for your dragon, who has fire inside him, we are all missing the warmth of Reylea. This world is harsh and bitterly cold. Nothing like our home."

"You don't all run hot like Col? He barely seems to notice the snow," Naomi asked, pulling her face away from her man's chest. "I figured it was a Reylean thing."

Col shook his head. "Only a dragon *thing*."

"We're warmer in animal form, but as men, we are quite uncomfortable in this weather. We found these coats in a cabin, but once we have clothes of our own, I intend on returning them." Kann gestured to the big parkas he and Saul were wearing. Their legs were still bare, and their boots were not made for the snow.

"The closest town up the river is Mystery, but they didn't have any shopping I noticed. We'll probably have to go across the river and south to McKinley Park. There are several resorts there for tourists and an airport. They'll have supplies."

"We are very grateful for your help," Kann spoke again. "Navigating this land has been troublesome."

"We're almost inside Denali Park right now. It's not always covered in snow. This far inland, summer starts promptly in June, but it ends in September. Right now, we are smack dab in the middle of winter. And from what the locals told me before I came out here, it's been a rough one. At least, that's what my research turned up before I came here."

"You do not live here?" Saul asked, giving her an inquisitive raised eyebrow.

She shook her head. "I'm here for work. I live a *really* long way from Alaska."

"Alaska," Kann spoke again. "That is the name of this place?"

"Yes. And we're north of Mt. Denali," she answered. Hissing from behind her made her turn. The water on the stove was boiling over. She left Col's side briefly to put the noodles into the water and turn down the heat.

The front door flew open, allowing in an icy blast of air.

"She's coming!" Tor shoved the door closed behind him. It slammed with a bang that made her heart jump.

The other two shifters at the table all stood at once.

"What's going on? Who's coming?" She switched the heat off under the noodles. If they were leaving the cabin, she didn't want to be responsible for starting a fire. Col pulled her to his side, away from the stove. The tension in his sinewy arms was like taut steel cables.

"The female dragon. What did you call her, Sefa?" Tor pushed his big fur hood off. His long fiery red-orange hair fell well below his shoulders. His beard was trimmed short, but the color was the same as his hair. "She's right behind me."

A roar exploded from Col's chest, sending vibration rippling through Naomi's body. "Get out!" The command sent everyone into motion. Col whirled, picked her up, and carried her out the front door into the twilight. Once outside, he paused and breathed in deeply. All three of the other shifters froze just inside the cabin door. Naomi could hear their weight shifting on the floorboards. They hadn't outright called Col their leader yet, but every move they made since arriving had been dictated by him. They watched him for every cue.

The wind was tossing snow everywhere. Around them. Against them. The porch was covered with several inches. The sky wasn't a complete white out yet, but it was getting close. Naomi couldn't tell if it was fresh powder falling or if the wind was just mixing up the snow already on the ground.

Icy winds whipped through her curls, but she didn't feel particularly uncomfortable. The air was cold—bitterly so—but she didn't feel the burn. Not like she had when she'd first gotten to McKinley Park and headed north to this cabin across the river.

The changes Col had pointed out seemed to have truly taken hold in her body. She had a pair of sweatpants on with a hoodie. No thermals. No gloves. Just a pair of socks.

She was standing in the snow on the porch in her *socks*. "What are we waiting for?"

"Sefa," Col said. "I cannot kill her until I can see her."

Naomi grabbed Col's arm. "You can't leave me."

The other three shifters moved through the door to flank her on the porch. Her heart kicked against her ribs, and her pulse roared in her ears like a hurricane had taken up residence inside her head. She couldn't think past the fact that Col was going to leave her alone. He was going to fight the other dragon.

He could die.

"Col, please."

"I will not allow her to hurt you." Col glanced over her shoulder and snarled at the other men. Fangs bared. Eyes the color of molten gold. "Keep her back. Sefa dies this night."

A low rumble cut through the howl of the wind, but it wasn't coming from Col.

Naomi looked up. The sky straight ahead and above them was on fire. Her heart crawled into her throat. Her lungs refused to breathe. She couldn't move, couldn't think. Flames were racing toward the cabin, rushing toward her like a billowing storm of death. No one would survive *that*.

She tried to scream. Tried to run. Tried to do something. But her brain couldn't get her body to comply. Multiple sets of hands grabbed her and pulled her inside the cabin. Col's body changed in front of her in a split second, blacking out the gray-white sky with his ebony dragon form. His wings spread out in a wide arc.

The fire never reached her.

The other men had pulled her inside. She hit the floor with an unceremonious thud. But she wouldn't be stopped. Col was *hers*.

She scrambled to her feet.

Col leapt into the air, chasing and attacking the red female.

Naomi ran through the still-open door, back into the

whirling snow and bitter cold. "Col!" Her cry blew back into her face. "Col!"

"Naomi, he would want you inside. Out of sight," Tor's voice was a deep bass. She glanced back at him. His eyes flickering gold reminding her of the way Col's would change when his animal rose to the surface. The other two men stood silently. Their eyes also flickering, watching, waiting for her to make a move. Tor reached for her arm again, but she ran down the steps into the snow away from him. Away from all of them.

Col was all that mattered.

Her heart beat as though it would leap from her chest. She sucked in breath after breath of the cold frozen air, but it didn't affect her. It was like fire flowed through her veins.

Then everything stopped. Time stood still as she watched Col's black dragon form fall from the sky. He hit the ground over the rise of a hill. She couldn't see him. The sky remained empty. He wasn't getting back up. He wasn't leaping into the air. He was just ... gone.

Col.

Her lungs wouldn't inhale.

Her heart wouldn't beat.

Naomi fell to her knees in the snow. She'd lost him. He was gone. Her worst fears realized. She'd let herself love him. She'd let herself move forward. Look what it'd gotten her. *More pain. More heartache.* She screamed into the fury of the wind, but the sound was thrown back into her face, a futile cry of desperation that no one could hear. Fiery streams of tears ran down her cheeks, creating a sharp contrast to the bitter cold wind.

"Naomi!" Tor's deep voice slipped through the howl of the wind like a gentle whisper. Like he was miles away and she was only hearing the echo of his cry.

Nothing mattered anymore. She'd lost the man who'd made her feel alive. For two years she'd been a living shadow. And then Col had quite literally crashed into her life. Her pulse pounded in her head, drowning out the whisper of Tor's worry. She bent down, touching her forehead to her legs, weeping under the deafening and painful and torturing roar of her adrenaline and emotions. And something else ... something else was burning from deep inside. Like a fire had ignited in her veins.

A dragon bugled overhead.

Naomi looked up.

The red dragon circled and then banked in the grey sky. Turned toward her. The red leathery wings were a sharp and stunning contrast to the pure white and grey sky. Sefa was getting closer. Naomi could see the glow of the dragon's eyes. Feel the force of her wings as she dove toward the ground with the speed and agility of a hunting eagle.

A feline growl shook Naomi's body from behind. An enormous orange and black striped animal leapt in front of her, blocking the red dragon's first attempt to snatch her from the ground. The dragon's claws ripped through his hide and the tiger shifter screamed in pain. Then Sefa cast him away like an unwanted stuffed animal.

The red dragon turned on Naomi again.

There was nowhere to go. Nothing to do.

Sefa had won.

The red dragon dove again. Tor was down. The lions were too far away. Sefa's claw closed around Naomi's torso. Around her ribs. The claw around her got tighter, squeezing until it was difficult to breathe. Pain crept like spreading frost across the surface of her skin. Burning. Burning. Burning.

Her pulse stuttered, like a car engine that wouldn't turn over. Her stomach knotted. Her vision blurred, and the silence was deafening.

Then everything slipped away to black. A black she couldn't see any way to escape.

FOURTEEN

COL

Col groaned and rolled from his back to his side. The snow drifts were packed hard under his massive dragon body, like a sheet of unforgiving granite. His wings were pinned at an uncomfortable angle. Col lifted his head from the ground and opened his eyes. Everything was white. In every direction. He couldn't see even the few feet between his face and his feet.

The storm had intensified. He couldn't see Naomi. Couldn't hear her.

Mate. His whole body leapt to action. He clawed the rest of the way to his feet and swung his head through the swirling storm of snow.

The cabin had to be close. They hadn't flown far. How had Sefa knocked him out of the sky? How had she gotten the drop on him? He looked around again, hoping to see more than white. *Still nothing.* Where was the red dragon?

A bugle cry tore from his large muzzle, challenging her to finish the fight. She'd knocked him down. Why wasn't she coming back? He shook out his wings, ready to fly. Still no challenge. He tucked them back close to his body. His chest rattled with an unspent roar.

She wouldn't have given up this fast.

But she was ... gone?

A lion's call split through the fury of the snowstorm. Not a war cry, but a summons. Col lumbered toward the sound and bugled again. The screaming wind and churning snow made him blind.

A feline roar echoed from the distance again.

A few more steps through the fog of white.

Over and over this repeated. He would call out. The lion would reply. One foot in front of the next. Each step brought him a little closer to his Tribe.

Col trudged forward. Another lion roar echoed across the expanse, different this time. He was so focused on getting back to them, he barely noticed the soreness and bruising from his fall.

He caught the faint scent of Naomi's flowery soap and dipped his head lower, closer to the ground. His mate's scent was mixed in with the tiger's.

With the tiger's *blood.*

His stomach rolled. His nostrils flared, and fear plunged like a sharp talon into his chest, reaching all the way to his pounding heart. Deeper. Deeper. Deeper.

Tor was injured?

Where was Naomi? When had she come outside?

"Over here," a voice called out this time—the lion named Saul. "Tor's been injured."

He charged toward the voice. The lights of the cabin came into view. The rising panic released, and his pulse slowed. He'd smelled her. *She would be here. She had to be here.*

Col pushed back his dragon and shifted into his human form. He charged up the steps into the cabin, shoving past Saul. The door was still open. "Naomi? Where is Naomi?"

The tiger shifter was on the floor with an enormous row of bloody gashes along his bare chest.

Dragon claw.

Col had made that pattern on more than one enemy. "Where is she?" He scanned the cabin. Her scent was there, but she was *not*. He couldn't hear her.

"He stopped her the first time." Kann knelt next to Tor, holding a rag against the deepest gash, slowing the blood flow. "We were right behind him." Kann shook his head. "The female dragon picked your mate up before we could get to her. I'm sorry."

Col's gut wrenched. His vision blurred. His heart heaved and rolled and crashed in his chest, cutting off his air, his control, his will to live.

Gulping wordless breaths, he tried to fill his burning lungs with something that would bring back that will. But oxygen wasn't enough. All the air in Reylea and Earth and all the worlds wouldn't be enough without Naomi.

"We're going to find her." Saul's tone deepened with a command that echoed Col's father.

Father.

He'd never feel the strength of his father's arm around his shoulder again. Never feel the soft embrace of his mother. Never hear the sweet laugh of his sister. And now, Sefa had stolen Naomi too.

Bitch. Traitor. Murderer.

Anger grew and twisted and rose in his veins like the lava had risen through the ground of Reylea. Steady. Relentless. Unforgiving.

He wanted to tear her apart, limb from limb, wing from wing, spike from spike. His dragon would bathe in her blood and make sure she felt every excruciating moment of her long slow death. Then he would leave her carcass for the scavengers, just like he'd left her brother's.

He hurled himself toward the front door. Toward the swirling wind and snow. His mate was out there. Somewhere.

Hands locked onto his arms and pulled him back. "Stop!" Saul and Kann shouted together. "You can't track her in this. None of us can."

Col snarled and snapped and slipped free of their grasp. "I have to find her."

Only one step and they were on him again. "You have to wait. You won't do any good to Naomi if you go out and die in this storm." Kann's logic bounced off like a sword would glance off his scales.

No effect. Just like the cold. He was immune.

Naomi needed him. Now.

"Release me." Col's skin tightened and burned. The two shifters snarled, sounding more lion than man, but still refused to let him out the door. Refused to let him go after his mate.

He threw off Saul first, tossing the large man across the room. The lion shifter thudded against the log wall and fell to the floor with a groan. Col's hands partially shifted, growing long deadly talons, and he ripped at Kann, slicing through the flesh of the lion shifter's arm and shoulder like he would a fresh kill.

Kann stumbled away from Col, clutching at the jagged edges of the wounds. His face was tight with pain, but he didn't make a sound. Kann leaned against the front door, blood seeping between his fingers. Blocking his exit. Even bleeding, he still blocked Col's path.

Bleeding.

Col looked at the blood dripping to the floor. He smelled the fresh copper scent. His nostrils flared, and he clenched his fists, shifting them back to fingers. He stared from Kann's bloody shoulder to Tor's larger chest wound. Col's shoulders sagged.

"I lost her."

Saul stood up across the room. "And, we're going to get her back. The moment the wind lets up. We leave. Only then can we track her. Track them both."

"We can't navigate in this weather. You couldn't find the cabin without following our roars. How would we ever find a small human?"

"I lost her." The words came out again, more broken this time. The realization of the truth they spoke was filling his stomach with rocks. The white seething snow outside was as good as a cage. No matter which way he moved, he wouldn't be able to *go* anywhere.

Saul walked slowly to Col's side. "Help me move Tor to the couch. The warmth will help him heal faster." The lion shifter stood, waiting, watching. No fear showed in his eyes, only patience.

Col glanced back at Kann. The other shifter hadn't moved. The drops of blood on the floorboards had expanded to a small puddle, but Kann wasn't budging from blocking access to the closed door. *Determined little bastard.* As mad as he still was, he couldn't help but feel a small amount of admiration for Kann's courage. Kann and Saul. Even Tor had tangled with a dragon to try and save his mate. And what was he doing? Causing more injury. Refusing to listen to reason.

"You should wrap that." Col's voice was wooden and emotionless.

Kann's lips twitched before he spoke softly, "I will."

"I'm sorry."

Kann released a long sigh. "I know."

"I have to do something." Fear crawled up from the cold floor and wrapped its ugly fingers around his heart. He was helpless. Useless.

"Help Saul move Tor." Kann never broke eye contact.

Col walked over to Tor's body and grabbed the man's legs. Saul took Tor's shoulders and they lifted, moving him quickly to the long couch in front of the woodstove. The wounds weren't bleeding anymore. They were angry and raw, but already healing. In less than an hour, they would be completely closed.

"N-a-omi?" The tiger shifter coughed and tried to turn his head.

Saul put his hand on Tor's shoulder. "Naomi was lost. The red dragon took her. Rest, we will leave to find her once the storm lets up."

"I can go now." Tor tried to sit up and Saul pushed him back down.

"The storm is too heavy. We can't see. We can't scent. We have to wait."

"Damn." Tor sank back into the cushions.

Col walked to the corner of the cabin and pounded the wall with his fist. "I should've killed Sefa the same day I killed Jaha. If I'd just left Naomi in that other cabin and hunted the bitch down. None of this would've happened."

"You cannot know that for sure." Saul leaned closer to the woodstove and rubbed his hands together. "Every choice you made once you recognized the *soul call* was to keep Naomi safe. Never doubt that."

"It wasn't enough."

"You don't know that either." Saul turned to face Col, his expression solemn. "If the dragon female wanted her dead, she would've left her body here."

Col swallowed down the rock lodged in his throat. Saul was right. Naomi could still be alive, but it wasn't likely. "She seeks to punish me." He slowly turned away from Saul and back to the door where Kann stood quietly —still bleeding. "And she has found the perfect way to do so."

What better way to damn a dragon than to murder their mate...

NAOMI

NAOMI MOVED A LITTLE AND GROANED. Everything ached as though she'd been run over by a bus. Or a train. Or maybe something bigger. What was bigger than a train?

She opened one eye and then the other, slowly, gritting her teeth against the biting wind. Her bare hands burned. Her face burned. She couldn't tell if it was the heat her body was generating or the ice in the wind striking her bare skin. "Col," she tried to call out. Her voice was swallowed by the wind swirling around her. Snow fell or was being blown around her, whiting out any landscape.

Naomi stretched her foot out and gasped when it fell off the edge of wherever she was sitting. She yanked it back and breathed deeply, her heart clawing its way up into her throat. Was she up on top of something?

She was leaning against jagged stone. Cold. Hard. Dark. Beneath her was the same. No snow remained. Her body had melted the snow and ice away.

Naomi reached into the blinding white and felt nothing. Until the snow ceased, and the wind died off, she couldn't see, and couldn't move. Not yet. At least from where she was, the stone wall at her back blocked some of the sting of the wind.

Where was the dragon that had picked her up?

Had she just been dropped somewhere?

No. No. No.

How would anyone ever find her in *this*? She fought against the panic rising in her chest. The part of her that wanted to move around and do something. She was as good as blind now. The blowing snow blended into everything. The light in the gray-white soup was fading, meaning the sun was setting soon. How long had she been out here?

She could feel the cold ... but she wasn't cold. Whatever was heating her from the inside was keeping her from turning into an Alaskan popsicle.

Nothing like getting superpowers from the bite of a dragon.

Naomi wrapped her arms around her knees and hugged them close to her body.

Just stay still. For now.

It wasn't safe to move, not when she couldn't see her way to climb down off of whatever she'd landed on. She breathed slowly, hauling air into her lungs and then blowing it out again. In and out. Again and again. The panic that had been digging into her chest like dozens of icepicks retreated. The air came and went, easier and easier.

She could hold on.

Col would be looking for her. He could find her.

As soon as the snow let up.

CHAPTER
FIFTEEN

COL

Col leaned against the front window of the cabin. Darkness had fallen but the snow hadn't let up. Not in the least.

His dragon rumbled and thrashed inside him, still convinced the best course of action was the search. Blind or not, at least they'd be doing something besides just standing in this cursed cabin.

Sefa knew where he was. Why didn't she return? Was she waiting for him to come to her? Had something happened? Was she lost in this snow with his mate?

"Col," Kann called from behind him.

Col ignored the lion shifter and continued to watch out into the blackness.

"Col?"

"What?" He knocked over a small side table next to the window. The splintering wood soothed the seething dragon beneath, but only for a brief moment. His dragon wanted to kill. He wanted to kill. To destroy.

"You should eat something. We leave as soon as the storm stops." Kann held out a golden loaf of some kind of bread.

He had no desire to eat. His stomach clenched and rolled at the thought. All he needed was Naomi. Life would continue for him only after he had her back safely in his arms. If that was even possible. "Eat then. I am fine." He turned back to stare out the window. "Leave me alone."

Col stood at the window for what seemed like hours.

The others moved quietly around, behind him. Even Tor had gotten up from the couch and eaten a little bread. His wounds had closed and were healing nicely. In a few more hours nothing would remain but long scars, a permanent reminder of Sefa's claws.

"Why are you here? Why did you seek me out to begin with?" Col asked, looking away from the blackness outside for a moment.

"We are a tribal people, Col. Our entire culture. We survive together, or not at all. This was drilled into us as younglings. Now we have lost our whole world. We have all lost our families and friends. We are in this new world with no support. No way to know if what we are doing will call attention to us. Or put us in danger. No way of knowing if the natives on this world are like us or not. At least the old magick followed us through and we can speak their language."

Very true. If he hadn't been able to speak to Naomi, it

would've driven Col mad. He was very grateful for the old magick of Reylea.

The old stories, passed on from generations ago said that a magick-bender cast a spell on all of Reylea. Everyone with Reylean blood could speak any language spoken to them. It took a few minutes. Enough words had to be spoken first, but it worked without fail. All the tribes spoke different languages, but after the magick spell had been cast, everyone could speak ... everything.

Even here in this world, it'd continued for them. Naomi's language had come to him. If there were other languages in this world, he'd be able to assimilate them as well.

"Is it not strange for you to drop all the disagreements? Unless it was the time of the gathering, none of the tribes ever came within several miles of each other. Rarely did even our hunting grounds overlap." Col watched the darkness outside through the corner of his eye.

"Of course, it's strange," Saul said from his seat on the floor next to the wood stove. "It does not mean that it is not the right choice. We will not survive out here alone unless we just let our animals overtake us and live as beasts. Your mate is proof of that. There are *things* in this world we do not understand. So much exists here that did not on our world."

"Saul is right. We need a human to instruct us about the people here and their *machines*." Kann said the last word like it was painful.

Col agreed though. The *technology* Naomi had shown him so far was unlike anything from their world.

"Hunting and fighting isn't the right way here. We must change our ways. We must learn," Kann wrapped up what was left of the loaf of bread. He left the kitchen and returned to sit opposite Saul near the wood stove. His shoulder had also stopped bleeding. The wounds had closed, and the scars would be minimal.

"The weapons the humans use are strange and dangerous." Tor pulled himself into a more upright position on the couch. "We will not be successful here if we don't help each other. How can we protect our future mates and children without a tribe?"

Col raised an eyebrow at the tiger shifter's comment. He hadn't considered that far into the future. More mates. Children.

Would the children be shifters? Or would they be like Naomi? *Human?*

"Do you think we will be the last of our kind?" Col asked, keeping his tone low.

The other males met his gaze with silence. Obviously, they hadn't considered that possibility yet. Neither had he, until just now.

"You don't think our children will be shifters?" Kann asked, rubbing his chin thoughtfully. "I'd never considered that. Not that it matters. You found a soul mate. That means Fate's magick can find *us* soul mates as well. We will be patient. If our children are not shifters, then that is what Fate wishes."

"Listen," Tor said.

Col turned his attention to the tiger shifter. "What?"

"The wind," the tiger responded.

He turned back to the window. The snow had slowed.

It hadn't quit, but it was enough to see a difference between the earth and the sky. If it continued to die down, soon it would be a still landscape and he'd be able to use his excellent vision and sense of smell to track.

"Wait a few more minutes. See if it quits completely." Saul rose from the floor. He crossed the room to stand next to Col at the window. "If it does, we can shift and track from the ground, while you fly overhead."

His body vibrated with the need to move. To fly. To seek his mate. His dragon thrashed and fought for control. Fire burned in his veins. He would scorch the entire countryside if it helped him find Naomi.

He did as the lion shifter suggested. They'd cover more ground together than he could alone. "Thank you." Col's voice was gruff.

"I bled for your mate," Tor said, totally serious, "I think that qualifies us as family. My brothers would be so jealous if they knew I could call a dragon *brother*."

Col's heart clenched. He'd never had a brother. He and his sister had been the only children of his parents. Tor's claim moved a part of him deep inside. His sister had died. Tor's brothers were gone, most likely dead.

They were truly alone in this new world. No one would understand them better. No one would be able to watch their backs better. They *did* need each other. Now, he needed them. Naomi needed them.

"We are Tribe." Col's tone firmed. "Family."

Tor and Kann stood, moving to the door as well. "Family," they said together.

"Let us go get your mate, Son of Li'Vhram." Tor extended his arm.

Col clasped his wrist and nodded.

It was time. He couldn't wait any longer.

He released Tor and opened the door. The air was bitter, but the snow had calmed. The night was still and cold, lit by the familiar green and pink colored lights in the sky. Naomi had already told him it was a phenomenon called *Aurora Borealis.*

"I still haven't gotten used to the magick that flows through this sky at night," Kann grumbled. "It feels as though Fate herself is watching me."

"It is not magick." They continued to walk together down the steps into knee-high snow. "Naomi said they are just lights caused by the magnetic poles of the planet."

"The what?" Tor said.

"Do not ask me about their *science.* I merely repeat what Naomi said," Col answered.

The others nodded in agreement.

A moment later, Col stood facing two lions and a tiger. Kann and Saul were on the bigger side for an average Reylean lion shifter. Their shoulders were at chest height. Their fangs, upper and lower, extended past their lips. The manes around their neck and shoulders made them look twice as big as they really were.

Tor's tiger had the same oversized fang teeth, but no mane. Nearly every shifter on Reylea had them. Claws and fangs were the key to survival.

Without them, death would come quickly.

Instead of the lions' tawny golden coat, Tor's tiger was bright orange with a white undercoat and black stripes that helped him blend into the jungles of Reylea. Here, he was like a beacon. He wasn't as tall as the lions, but just as muscled and perhaps a few feet longer.

The big cats growled low and stretched their massive bodies. They waited for him. They were Tribe, family now, but they'd silently put him in place as their leader. At least for now.

Col shifted and let out a loud trumpeting cry into the now-clear night air. His dragon roared and then he swung his head down toward the cats. His body was enormous comparatively, but they were still formidable enemies—allies now.

Sefa would die today.

COL HAD BEEN FLYING for several hours. The scent trail was getting stronger. The female dragon wasn't hiding, and he could pick out Naomi's light floral scented soap on the edge of the wind.

They were heading due south toward the high snow-capped peaks. Better hiding for a dragon. Flight negated the difficult terrain, but it would be problematic for his companions below.

He banked and turned, scanning the ground hundreds of feet below him. The three cats were still moving at a breakneck pace, churning through the snow and up over the foothills below him.

With allies, Naomi would be protected on the ground while he ended Sefa once and for all.

The Aurora Borealis floated and twisted around him as he flew. It'd been strange when he'd encountered it the first night. Naomi had assured him it was harmless and merely a light in the sky, like a flame without heat.

Sefa's scent was stronger now, but still, nothing. No movement in the sky or on the ground except for the three cat shifters. Further and further they traveled. The air became thinner and clearer. The cats below had slowed a little. To his surprise they were doing an excellent job of keeping up with his pace. He wasn't flying at full speed, but he wasn't lazing along either.

A dark shadow above him caught his eye, however not fast enough to evade Sefa's dive. She was using his own move against him. Again.

Her shoulder caught his back just above his wing base.

Col roared and fell from the sky. One of his wings still worked, but it wasn't enough to stay airborne. The aggressive move had left Sefa in a free fall also. He watched with arrogant satisfaction as she struggled to slow her descent only a short distance from him.

They would both hit soon.

The ground was rising fast, but nevertheless he would survive the impact. Likely, they both would. The snow cushioned his fall more than he'd counted for, allowing him to recover his feet.

Col lunged to where the female dragon lay sprawled and dazed.

The three cat shifters were circling but hadn't attacked, leaving justice for him to dispense.

She had murdered his family.

She had stolen his mate.

She would die.

Right.

Now.

He spewed flames to blind her and used his strong back legs to launch himself at her. Their bodies slammed together. Her claws sought his belly, but he was faster.

They rolled down a hill, through several groves of trees. Biting and slashing. The wounds Sefa inflicted were shallow and of no account.

Col ripped into her, tearing spikes from her back with his jaws. Her blood was sweet in his mouth. His claws shredded her wings.

She wouldn't be able to escape or limp away this time.

His jaws clamped down on one of her forelegs and he didn't release her until the bones crunched between his teeth. She screamed, and his dragon howled for more.

End her.

She rolled away from him, and he leaped again, giving her only seconds of a reprieve before breaking another of her legs. Sefa was immobile now. Bleeding and staining the white ground red.

He stood on her neck, holding her down and tore a long gash from her neck to her tail with his back claw. Blood sprayed into his face. Her cries fed his need for vengeance more than justice.

Col's dragon reared back to strike her neck and finish her when she shifted to her two-legged form. Into a woman.

Surprised, his dragon took a step back.

Sefa was clothed in a red tunic that quickly became soaked with blood from her numerous wounds. Then she spoke, her voice filled with bitterness and arrogance.

"You may have won, Son of Li'Vhram, but you will suffer eternally." Her eyes flashed with anger and satisfaction.

Col held back the death strike and shifted to stand next to her.

What did she mean?

"If your mate isn't dead yet, she will be before you can find her. I crushed her and threw her at the top of that mountain. You will feel nothing but emptiness and pain for the rest of your long life. You will know I took your mate from you just like your father took away my mother. That my family took everything..." Her breathing slowed. Blood dripped from her mouth. Sefa coughed and spit out more. "You h-have n-nothing ... because of me." Her eyes glazed over, and the life in them disappeared completely. Red spread out on the white snow like a crimson cloak.

He was standing in her blood. Could feel the sticky warmth of it as it melted through the snow at his clawed feet. *That's what the attack had been about? His entire family had died because Sefa's* mother had gone mad. Execution had been the only option to protect the tribe. Now Sefa had died for her part in murdering his entire family. For taking Naomi. Killing his mate, but could she be alive? The smallest sprout of hope blossomed in his heart. Sefa had not watched Naomi die.

She could still be alive.

The mountain. She said she threw her to the mountain.

Col turned. The peak in the distance was huge. Higher than any mountain he'd seen in Reylea. It was sharp and jagged, and his mate was there.

Alive or dead. He would find her.

CHAPTER
SIXTEEN

NAOMI

Naomi struggled to breathe.

In and out. You can do this.

The wind still whipped around her, but the snowstorm had cleared. She peeked an eye open and wished she hadn't. Her stomach crawled up into her mouth and threatened to leap to its death at the bottom of the mountain.

Holy fucking shit.

The entire Denali snowcapped range lay before her.

No. No. No.

Shadows of white peaks and colored snow reflected the northern lights. Except she couldn't see Mt. Denali. All the ridges around her seemed to be below her.

Her oxygen-starved brain finally caught up. *Because you're fucking on top of Mt. Denali!*

She wasn't on the peak—more like stuck on a ridge on the side. Tucked into a cranny with nowhere to go. It was light enough with the stars and the Aurora Borealis in the sky to see there wasn't a way up or down from the little ledge of jagged rock she was sitting on.

A fucking mountain. It had to be the top *of a fucking mountain.*

It was good it was dark. Naomi couldn't see quite how far down it was. Only a guess. It helped keep her fear from completely shutting her brain down, not that it didn't have its fingers poised right on the buttons that would completely paralyze her. It did. She could feel the claws tapping in her brain, waiting, watching. She could freak out at any moment. Completely lose it.

But she hadn't yet.

Still, her body was tight, and she could barely draw in tiny breaths. The mountain was high, higher than she'd ever been before. Her head still hurt. Her skin hurt. Everything hurt.

Pain like someone had stabbed her, wrapped itself around her chest. Even the small puffs of air she managed hurt. She rubbed the back of her head and felt warm wet liquid. She was bleeding. She'd hit her head.

Her shirt was wet too. She touched her side and then lifted her fingers to her lips. *More blood.*

Her skin still felt like it was on fire, like she was burning from the inside out. It was similar to the feeling she had after Col had first bitten her, but that fever had burned off in a day and she'd been fine. This one felt as though it would consume her completely.

"Col," she called, disappointed that her voice was barely louder than a whisper, and as hoarse as an old woman who'd smoked her whole life.

She tried again and got a little more out the second time. "Col!" Naomi managed to give a decent scream the third time. Her voice echoed off the peaks and a rumble like thunder sounded above her.

Fucking shit.

Bits and pieces of snow fell from above her onto her head. She held her breath and waited for more. The thunder faded and nothing else happened.

She brushed the snow from her curls and coughed. Pain flared, and she whimpered. Her ribs were cracked. They had to be. Or broken.

No more screaming. Got it.

How was she supposed to get down from here? Would Col even come looking this far? They were hundreds of miles from the cabin where she'd been staying just north of McKinley Park. Damn dragon.

She would feel better if she could just stand up and get a better look at where she was. It was so hard to see in the dark.

She put her hands on the rock face behind her and carefully pushed herself up until she was standing. Her legs ached and hurt, but nothing seemed to be broken. Naomi wobbled and caught herself.

Her heart climbed into her throat to join her stomach and she closed her eyes. Now was not the time to have a panic attack. *Well, it is. You're at the top of a fucking mountain, but if you want to live ... you won't.*

There had to be a way down the mountain. Other than falling off the ledge, that was. She pulled in a slow breath and tried to get past the lightheadedness and nausea and pain. God, the pain was so bad. It reminded her of that time she'd had a full body sunburn when she was fifteen and had dragged her best friend to the beach. Her poor skin had actually peeled that summer.

Naomi felt along the ledge with her foot and inched her way to the right. No luck. The ledge she'd been sitting on was getting narrower and narrower. The edge was now right behind her foot. She turned her head, pressing her cheek to the cold granite wall.

Baby steps.

A few minutes later, she made it back to the wider part of the ledge, and then continued past it to see if it changed on the other side. Instead of getting narrower it just stopped.

Another wall of granite blocked her view and her ability to continue moving. She turned around and slid her back slowly down the wall in the corner, since it was the widest. Naomi could stretch her legs out in front of her here and they didn't hang out into the open air.

After a moment of sitting and dragging in one breath after another. The altitude, plus her panic wasn't doing her any favors. She turned on her side and lay down. The stone was cold at first, but within a few moments her body heat had warmed it. If only she had a blanket to keep off the cold bite of the arctic wind, or at least a pillow to ease the loud throbbing in her head.

"Yeah, cause a blanket and pillow would really fix everything, Naomi." She mocked herself quietly. "What you really need is a damned dragon."

COL

THE THREE MALES shifted back to their two-legged forms and approached Col.

"We can still find her. Her scent is in the wind." Kann turned and pointed south toward the mountain range. "Sefa said she dropped her there."

Col quelled the beast in his chest. His dragon couldn't help him right now. It'd be several hours before his wing had healed enough to carry him again. "I cannot fly. Sefa injured one of my wings."

"I'll carry you until it mends." Saul shifted back to his lion form and went to Col's side, then bent his forelegs down.

Col took hold of the thick mane, put a foot on the bent foreleg and swung himself up onto the lion's back. He crouched down and bent his legs, hugging to Saul's sides. "Thank you." He looked over at Tor and Kann.

They nodded and shifted back into their cat forms.

Saul started slowly, allowing Col to adjust to the feel of his lion's stride, then ran faster and faster. His legs ate up the snowy ground and the mountains grew closer.

Naomi's scent grew stronger.

They climbed up and down the lowland hills, each higher than the last.

Saul breathed hard beneath Col's body. The great lion's sides heaved with exertion, and yet he continued on.

For him. For his mate.

They were working as a united team. A Tribe.

He pointed at the top of a rise just to their left. Naomi's scent was even stronger.

The three cats veered to the left, following his prompting as a single unit. The sky was black and filled with stars and swaths of colors. The low light made traveling easier than if it was pitch dark, but Col still wished for the light of the sun. His long-distance vision was being wasted in the darkness.

Tor dropped to his belly at the top of the next hill.

The two lions slowed to a crawl and moved slowly on their bellies until they were even with Tor at the edge of the ridge.

Col strained in the dark to see, but he couldn't make out anything.

Then the scent hit him full on.

Wolves.

The next question was—wolves from earth or wolves from Reylea?

Tor shifted into a man to speak. "Stay here, I'm going to get a little closer. If they are Reylean, we can't chance going down this ridge. Last time we saw a group of wolves, there were at least ten."

"Be careful." Col breathed out the warning without hesitation, surprised to find that he actually cared a great deal about what happened to the other man.

The tiger nodded, shifted back into animal form and slunk into the darkness. In the dark, his coloring gave him the ability to move across the snow like a shadow, his stripes blending into the trees and low growing brush.

Minutes stretched.

A wolf howled.

Then another.

And another.

They'd spotted Tor. Or scented him.

Either way, Col wasn't going to let his companion get torn apart by a group of bloodthirsty wolves.

Wolves killed because they liked it. Even on Reylea, they'd kill stragglers or loners just for the fun of it. Slowly and cruelly. They enjoyed inflicting pain, and everyone hated them for it.

He leaped from Saul's back and started running down the ridge into the small valley. He shifted, taking even bigger strides with his dragon form.

Trees crunched beneath his claws. He roared, shaking the air with his anger.

A wolf charged at him from the right. A quick spray of fire ended his attack in a scream of rage and then pain. Then silence.

Col didn't stop. He just kept running. They knew he was a dragon. If they really wanted to challenge him, they would *all* die.

Tor roared and fell into pace beside him.

Col stopped, took a deep breath and shot out an arc of flame longer than his body, ahead into the forest. He swung his head wide and a huge swath of the trees burned bright like a thousand torches had been lit all at once.

After the flames were soaring into the night sky, he roared, snarling and snapping at the air with his massive jaws.

Let them come.

They'd feel nothing but his wrath.

A few yelps and howls echoed through the air. But not a single wolf approached.

Saul and Kann trotted to stand next to Tor.

Col swung his head around to look down at the large cats. He flicked his tongue and tasted the air. Ash. Shifters. *Naomi.* Her scent filled the breeze coming from down the mountain.

Her blood. That was new.

He growled and took off running, plowing his way through the burning trees. Even if he couldn't fly, he'd get to her. He'd climb the entire mountain claw by claw if that was what it took.

Trees snapped in his path as he tore through the forests and climbed. Col flapped his wings just to see if they'd lift him. He managed a few feet of gliding before the pain was too much. He needed more time to heal. The wing wouldn't stay extended.

They were past the foothills now and climbing up the side of the snowcapped peak. The one his mate had called Deh-nah-lee. It was so high. Higher than any mountain in Reylea. The highest in the whole of the range surrounding him right now. Her blood was stronger in the wind now. It didn't matter how high. Or how far. He had to get to her. She could still be alive.

She could.

He hoped and wished and prayed to the gods of every world that would listen.

Kann and Saul galloped next to him on his right. Tor kept pace on his left.

Harder.

Faster.

They all pushed their animals to the limit of their abilities. His heart pounded. His legs burned. Col wasn't used to running and his short legs and massive claws weren't meant for this kind of distance. Quick leaps or sprints were easy, but he'd run for miles now. His lungs burned from sucking in the cold air.

It didn't matter. His *shuarra* was injured. Hurting. Scared...or dead.

Failure was not an option. He would find her.

NAOMI

Naomi woke with a start and screamed. The pain was worse. Her head felt as though it were splitting open. Her skin still burned. She writhed back and forth on the narrow stone ledge on the side of the mountain, trying to breathe through it, but her lungs stuttered and gasped. Her heart skipped, and the moment she finally managed to gulp in a breath of air, the bottom of the ledge fell out from under her, like that horrible dream in the middle of the night that people never grew out of.

Falling.

Weightless.

Lost.

The seconds ticked by. She couldn't breathe. Couldn't see. Everything was rushing. Her heart. The wind around her. Only the sky was a constant. As she fell, the sky didn't change. She watched the beautiful colored lights ripple across the inky blackness.

She had a strange sense of calm wash over her being. Almost like someone was there with her. Which was ridiculous. She was alone. Falling to her death off the side of a mountain. But still, the panic didn't take over.

The pain in her head faded as she fell.

Her skin no longer burned.

Her ribs didn't hurt.

Thud. Her back met the pillow of snow on the ground like a bus that'd gotten shoved off a freeway overpass. Every tiny, microscopic ounce of air was knocked from her lungs. She wanted to move. Wanted to breathe. Wanted anything other than to be frozen on her back unable to draw breath.

Maybe she was dying?

Finally, her lungs unlocked, and she gulped for air. Her lungs felt as though they were as big as cars. Her breath just kept going and going. Air had never felt so good.

Not dying. At least not yet.

Her thundering heart slowed as her inhales and exhales found a lengthier rhythm. She opened her eyes and looked up at the sky. It was the same as before. Dark. Full of colorful lights. Beautiful. She looked up at the side of the mountain from where she'd fallen. Then her gaze drifted down just a hair and she stared at what looked like a dragon's claw sticking straight up into the night sky.

She groaned and tried to move.

The leg moved too.

The claws contracted.

Her body felt so heavy. So huge.

She waved her hand, except it was a claw that moved again.

Her stomach churned and heaved and didn't know which way the fuck to climb.

She gasped again and froze when the sound that came from her throat wasn't ... human. Her heart thundered, harder and louder than before. Like she had a whole heavy metal rock band inside her chest.

Holy shit. I'm a dragon.

She screamed again, and this time the call was unmistakably exactly like the bugle cries she'd heard out of Col.

I really am a dragon.

She blinked and stared up at the night sky. Her vision zoomed, like she'd turned a dial on a telescope. The Aurora Borealis was brighter ... or closer? And, *damn,* it was almost like she was up in the Milky Way.

She couldn't tell. Then her vision changed again, backing up like she'd turned a dial on a pair of binoculars. Now she could see the whole mountainside stretching before her and the valley between this mountain and the next.

She rolled to the side and struggled to get her feet beneath her—all four of them. Being a dragon certainly explained why the fall *didn't* kill her, but coordination was going to be an issue.

A yellow light glowed in the distance, catching her attention.

Fire?

How could anything be on fire out on the side of a mountain ... *unless. Col!*

Mate. An unfamiliar voice in her head spoke. *Find mate.*

Yes, she very much wanted Col. Her mate.

Naomi took a step forward and fell flat on her stomach. Her head turned ... or rather *swung* to the side. A part of her she didn't recognize was moving ... behind her. She could feel snow swishing back and forth. Naomi turned to look over her shoulder and belched out a cry of shock. She shouldn't have been surprised to see a tail. Col had a tail. She moved her head, surprised by the angle she could achieve. She had spikes up and down her back, just like Col too. She wasn't black, though. Even in the semi-darkness, she could tell the color of her scales were different from his.

She moved her tongue and it flicked between her lips. *Really big teeth.*

I really am a dragon. This happened.

Yes. The unfamiliar voice called from inside her again.

She lifted her arm and peered through the darkness at a massive, clawed foot.

Ohmygod!

Naomi put that foot down and lifted another. Her entire body was a novelty. The wind still whipped around her body, but she didn't feel the cold at all now except when she breathed. None of her previous injuries seemed to remain. The slashes on her torso or the gash on her head. Either that, or they were so small while she was in this form, they were non-issues.

Mate. The voice called out again.

Right. Col.

She needed to get back to Col.

What about Sefa? She could barely walk. What would happen if the female dragon came back for her right now? She wouldn't stand a chance.

Fly. The voice urged.

Hell, to the no!

She swung her head around again, just to check. Sure enough, she had enormous wings tucked tightly against her side. No way was she even going to attempt flying. It'd been bad enough with Col carrying her. She was deathly afraid of heights. She'd get off this mountain, but she was doing it on *four* legs.

No flying for her. Dragon body or not.

She clambered through the snow clumsily, trying to figure out how to balance her huge body. Her tail was helping a little, but it felt so strange. Then there was her head and long neck that kept rocking back and forth with every step making her seasick.

A grove of tall spruce trees blocked her way forward. She pushed her chest through the first few and winced as they snapped with each step.

This was the quickest way down the mountain, and the quickest way back to Col.

The cabin where she'd been staying was miles and miles north of Mt. Denali. That bitch of a female had carried her a *long* way.

How would Col ever be able to find her?

A loud trumpeting cry spilled out of her as the desire to cry became overwhelming. Then another. And another.

Naomi pushed through the last few trees and came to another open snowy space. She was moving faster now, having found some semblance of coordination between her four limbs. The mountain just kept going. Further and further down. She must've really been nearly at the top of the twenty-thousand-foot peak.

A trumpeting call from her left made her slide to a very ungraceful stop, meaning her legs folded underneath her, sending the rest of her rolling several times before she was able to stop and right herself.

Light from the approaching sunrise was chasing away some of the shadows, turning the blackness to a lighter gray. Her vision narrowed in on movement along the top of a ridge.

The view changed and suddenly she was seeing the ridge magnified at least ten times. *Very cool ability.* There on the ridge charging toward her was Col—in dragon form—and the other shifters she'd met too.

Holy crap! Those were big cats. She remembered seeing Tor change into a tiger just before Sefa had grabbed her, but the lions too were slightly bigger than average too and had fangs like some kind of prehistoric saber-tooth. They were all as scary as fuck. Of course, she was one of them now ... wasn't she?

She was like Col. His bite had changed her. All the pieces fit together. The fever. The way her skin hurt and burned. All that pain had been her body changing ... shifting to what she was now. Falling off the ledge. She'd started to change and when she had ... she'd fallen.

They were getting closer now. They weren't slowing down. Would Col recognize her?

He wouldn't think she was the other female, would he? Panic set in and she started backing up. She could run. Well, attempt to run. Though she probably couldn't keep up with a deer at her level of coordination.

Please know me.

She made a low whining sound and crouched to the ground, instinctively trying to protect her belly.

Please know me.

She closed her eyes and waited.

COL

Col raced toward the trumpeting dragon. It had Naomi with it somewhere. Her scent was all over it. Sefa and Jaha hadn't been alone?

How had he missed *another* female? He charged forward, checking his sides.

The cats were still keeping up with the grueling pace he'd set.

When he'd heard the first bugle cry, his dragon had nearly lost it. He'd tried to fly again but still couldn't.

Frustrated, he'd pushed himself even harder, climbing the foothills to the snow-covered mountainside at a pace that had him panting for air and his heart kicking against his ribs.

The darkness had changed to a light gray.

The unfamiliar dragon was ahead, backing away slowly like it was scared. She was hunched low in the snow and her wings were still firmly entrenched against her back. Why wasn't she fleeing?

Then again, why had she called out? Surely, she knew he'd come for his mate. That he would kill any who got in his way.

She trumpeted again, a strange call that sounded more like a cry of fear than a challenge.

He stopped abruptly and snarled at the cats, warning them off. They were still out of fire range, but if they kept going, they wouldn't be. A scared dragon meant unpredictability. He huffed at them and shook his large head. They nodded and backed off a few steps, understanding his request.

Col continued forward. The female wasn't raising her wings. She wasn't growling or being aggressive. If anything, her body language said she was cowering.

Where was Naomi? Her scent covered this new female. What had she done with her? She was right to cower because he'd beat her until she shifted and told him where his mate was.

He wouldn't make the same mistake with this one like he had with Sefa. Wouldn't kill her quickly. Not until he had answers.

Mate. His dragon roared inside his head.

He bellowed out a challenge cry, but the female didn't move.

Her sleek head was barely above the snow. Her bright yellow eyes were watching his every move. Was Naomi's body beneath her? Was that why she was hovering over the snow, moving so slow?

The female made a low whine and shook her head back and forth.

No challenge.

She wasn't going to fight?

He roared, his frustration building.

The other dragon backed up a few more steps, fear evident in its wide flashing eyes. Gold swirled with brown, and it made the strange whining sound again.

Col stalked forward, his gaze stuck to the snow she'd uncovered. No Naomi. No sight of her anywhere, except her scent covered the ground.

She was here. Or had been here.

He shifted to his human form and kept walking toward the female. It was a risk. She could kill him more easily in this from, but his gut said she wasn't going to attack. "Where is she? Where is Naomi? What did you and Sefa do with her?"

The dragon's head tilted at his words. She made a pitiful sound, worse than the whining.

"Where is my *shuarra?* I will kill you for hurting her," he bellowed.

The female's head pulled back with a jerk of surprise and she backed up a couple more steps.

"Show me my mate! Are you holding her?" Col maneuvered, trying to see if the dragon had a body in one of its large claws. He couldn't tell. The snow was so deep. He was struggling to stay on top of the powder as it was.

He breathed deeply, trying to calm the fire and anger bubbling beneath the surface. Naomi had been here. Her scent was so strong. So sweet. It was everywhere.

The female dragon stood quietly as he circled around to her left, slowly scanning the trees. Her tailed whipped back and forth without consequence, like that of a youngling who had not been trained. She was all gold and bronze, her scales smooth and glassy without a single mark. He didn't recognize her ... at all. She was not from his Tribe.

Who was she?

Her head swung over her back, and she continued to watch him, quietly now. No whine. No growl. Just an intense stare.

Col's stomach dropped to his feet, all air rushed from his lungs, and his heart did a somersault inside his chest. How could he have missed it?

"Naomi?" He met the dragon's gaze.

The female visibly sighed and sank into the snow, releasing all the tension and fear she'd been holding onto. She swung her head low, inching it closer and closer to him, until she was nudging his hands with her snout.

"My *shuarra*, I didn't realize." His bite had changed her. Made her like him?

Naomi was a dragon... Naomi was a dragon!

His heart soared with relief and excitement and guilt all at the same time.

She was alive. She was a dragon. He hadn't lost his mate.

Col had changed her without her permission. He hadn't known it would happen. He'd needed to mark her. Needed to bond their souls. He hadn't known it would change her so completely. "I—" he started. "Forgive me, *shuarra*. I would've asked first, if I had known what my bite would do."

The dragon nodded her head up and down, butting him softly in the side with her lips.

"Shift for me, my love." He kept his voice soft. Coaxing.

Naomi shook her big bronze-colored head and made the whining sound again.

Could she not shift?

He studied her carefully and thought. As younglings, they had to learn to control the animal within. Find a balance that could be shared by both halves of the soul.

Naomi wouldn't have that training.

He put a hand on her snout and rubbed her warm glassy scales.

She stopped whining.

"Listen to me, my *shuarra*. You must think of your body as you wish it to be. The dragon is part of you. She will listen to your desires. I am here. I will never leave you again. You are beautiful Naomi. Sleek and strong and perfect in this form, but I wish to hold you in my arms.

The dragon in front of him disappeared in an instant.

In the center of the space where the large body had been, his mate sat curled in the snow. Tears ran down her tawny cheeks. Her brown eyes were ringed with red. Exhaustion. Fear. So much poured from her.

"Col!" she wailed. She stretched out her arms and he shoved his way through the slushy snow and plucked her naked body from the ground.

He buried his face in her hair, then in her neck, breathing in her scent, assuring himself and his dragon that they had her back. That she was safe and whole and once again where she belonged—at his side.

"God, Col I was so scared. I woke up on a ledge at the top of the mountain. I started to change and fell off. Then all the pain disappeared. And I realized I was a dragon."

"What pain, my *shuarra?*"

"My skin was on fire. It was so bad I wanted to rip it off. And then my head hurt. Pounded so hard, like something was bashing it in with a rock. Then I fell and it all disappeared."

"You didn't realize you had shifted?"

"Not until I tried to move around a little."

Col nuzzled her neck again and squeezed her tighter.

"Forgive me. I wouldn't have—"

She stopped him with a soft finger across his lips. Her eyes held only love for him. No hatred or disgust or anger. "You already have my forgiveness, my mate." Naomi shook her head. "There is nothing else that must be said. I know you would've given me a choice if you had known. And if I'd had that choice, Col, I would've chosen you. I will always choose you."

His heart slowed in his chest. Air came more easily.

She didn't hate him. She wasn't angry that he'd turned her into a dragon. She wanted him. Naomi was his mate in every way.

A smile curved his lips,, and he claimed her mouth. Hers were warm and soft and damp. Wanting. Needing.

She welcomed his tongue and claim. His heart thudded against his ribs like a war club. *His.* She was intoxicating. A soft whimper came from her throat, and he growled against her mouth, taking the kiss deeper. Harder.

Mate. His dragon crowed from within, pleased that Naomi was safe. That she was in his arms. That her familiar taste and scent covered his lips.

"I never thought I was going to see you again." Emotion poured down her cheeks in rivers of pain and relief and hope. "I thought—"

"You are safe now. Sefa is gone." Col gestured to the three large cats standing off to the side a short distance away. "They helped me find you."

"So, the new tribe is a go?" she asked, a twinkle of pleasure in her brown eyes.

"A go?"

"It's happening. We're not going to go off and live in a cave all by ourselves? We get to have other people around. Like a family." The tone of her voice was filled with excitement.

He had been prepared to isolate her. His beautiful mate who'd told him so many things about her own large family. How important they were to her.

She'd practically ordered him to allow Kann and the others inside the cabin to talk. How had he not seen it?

Had he been so blinded by his own problems that he couldn't see the way she'd been begging to not be alone? Even still, Naomi would've chosen him. She would've lived in a cave, alone and sad, with him if that'd been what he'd asked of her...guilt bloomed in his chest like a fire out of control.

"*Shuarra,* yes." Col looked at the shifters again, still in their animal forms. Still waiting. "We will work together as a tribe. We will not be alone. I will never let you be alone."

"I LOVE YOU, COL." She nuzzled her face against his chest. He'd just given her everything she could ask for. They'd have other Reyleans around them.

A tribe all together.

Naomi didn't have to be alone and isolated. Especially now that she was one of *them*. She wasn't Reylean, but she was a dragon shifter now. Whatever came along with that. It would be good to have other shifters around besides just Col.

"You are my heart, Naomi. I love you more than I have loved anyone or anything in my entire life." He hugged her closer.

Kann shifted and came forward. He removed his coat and held it out to Col. "For your mate."

"Thank you, brother," Col said.

Kann's eyes widened, and a smile curved his lips. "Brother," he returned, and gave Col a quick nod before returning to where Tor and Saul stood, still in animal form.

"We really shouldn't be animals during the day. This is a national park. There are campers and hikers all over this park. If they see a lion or tiger on the slopes, we would be in all kinds of trouble. Dragons are definitely a no-go until dark." Naomi took the coat from Col and slipped into it.

She was short enough that all the important bits were covered. All the way down to her knees. No shoes and no pants would still be suspicious to any passing humans. Plus, the fact that she was traveling with four dudes who were dressed like Dothraki warriors from Game of Thrones.

"My wings are still healing, but I should be able to fly by the time night falls again. The sun is not right here. The days seem shorter."

"Yeah, we are really far north on the planet. The daylight is really skewed here. Changes with the seasons. Sometimes there is no night. And other parts of the year, no day."

Col's eyebrows scrunched together, but he didn't say anything just nodded and helped her tie the last of the fasteners on the coat.

The other three men had come closer, and Kann spoke again.

"If it is not safe to travel during the day, should we look for shelter and then head for the cabin once the sun sets again?" The lion shifter rubbed his arms and gave the surroundings a cursory glance.

Naomi felt really guilty about taking his coat. She didn't need the warmth, but she also couldn't walk around buck naked around other dudes.

Col wouldn't let her, even if she was willing.

"They aren't going to last long dressed like that. The temps when I arrived were falling to negative thirty at night. Day isn't going to be much better." She glanced at Kann and the others again. "We need to dig a shelter. And get a fire started."

"How do you know to do this?" Col asked her as they walked over to Saul and Tor.

"I read a lot before I came. I was scared if I got stuck outside, I'd freeze to death, so I read a bunch of survival guides." Naomi scanned their surroundings.

They weren't off the mountain yet, but they were low enough that some of the foothills had created a rise. Which is why she'd stopped rolling, at least, that was what she assumed.

She pointed to a flat area. "We need to pile snow there. Into a big mound. Pat it down and then hollow it out like an animal would for a burrow. It needs to be big enough for all of us to fit inside and to light a fire in the center."

The three men looked around then shifted into their cat forms.

Naomi gulped. They were big. Not like Jurassic Park big, but certainly bigger than the average lion or tiger she'd seen in the zoo.

The lions and tiger bounded down the hillside a few dozen yards and began digging. They used their large paws to move the snow into a central mound between them.

"I should help." Col pulled her along toward the growing mound, and then sat her on a fallen tree before shifting into his dragon.

With his enormous claws, he shoveled snow onto the mound until it was taller than Saul. All four men shifted back to human form and started patting down the snow until it was firm enough to walk on. The resulting mound was easily ten feet tall.

"The entrance should be as narrow as possible. Less wind. Then dig it out once you're in the center. We need a branch to poke down through the top, so you know where the middle is when you get there."

The men nodded and continued to work on firming up the mound.

Naomi wandered over to the area where she'd crawled up out of the snow. There were lots of broken tree trunks strewn about. She yanked at one and was surprised to find that it moved several inches.

Look at me all super-strong-dragon-lady.

She pulled again, and the trunk moved again.

"Naomi." Col was at her side a few moments later. "Why are you over here? By yourself?" he asked, his tone a mixture of worry and annoyance.

"I said we needed a branch. I just wanted to help," she answered. "It's not like I was out of sight or even earshot."

He batted the tree trunk away and pulled her into his arms. "I just got you back. Don't wander. Not yet. When I turned and didn't see you, it felt as though someone had stabbed me in the heart."

She started to argue then she saw the pain and worry reflected in her mate's eyes. He wasn't trying to be controlling, like her brothers. It wasn't that he didn't want her help or think she was incapable of helping, like her dad who thought women only belonged in the kitchen.

Col was worried about her safety. She couldn't fault him for that.

"I can help," she said slowly. "I'm strong now."

He kissed the top of her head and then rumpled her curls. "Of course, you are my *shuarra*. You are Dragon

Tribe. But I need more than an hour to settle *my* dragon and assure him that you aren't going to disappear or be stolen away again."

Naomi smiled up at her dragon man. "My big barbarian. I love you. You know that."

"Yes." He gave her a smug smile, stole a quick kiss, and then grabbed the end of the tree trunk she'd been excavating with one hand and her with the other. "What is the next step for the snow tent?"

She laughed and hurried ahead of him a few steps to the edge of the enormous mound of snow. "You have to drive it down in the middle. Then dig toward it from the very edge."

The men considered her for a moment, and then hurried to follow the instruction.

Kann and Col drove the trunk down the center from the top.

Saul started to dig an entrance and Naomi helped by moving the snow from behind him each time he pushed an armful out.

"We need short sticks, about two feet long." She gestured the size with her hands. "They go into the roof, so you don't clear out too much snow and have it fall in."

"You stay." Col growled a warning before she could leave the entrance to go look. "Kann and Tor will get them."

The two other men nodded and hurried over to the closest grove of birch trees. She returned to pushing off the snow Saul was clearing out as he tunneled toward the center trunk.

"Got it!" Saul backed his way out and turned to face Naomi.

"We need the sticks next." She pointed to Tor and Kann who were walking back to the snow mound each with an armful of sticks. "They need to be this long." She motioned the size again, showing Saul and Col.

Kann and Tor dropped the sticks at the base of the mound.

All five of them broke them into the desired length and Naomi showed them how to stick them into the mound all over.

A smile broke out on Saul's face. "The ends will poke through if we dig too far," he exclaimed, moving even faster.

They quickly had the *snow tent* staked and ready.

Saul crawled back in first and went to town clearing out more of the mound.

Naomi and the others moved pile after pile of snow from the narrow entrance.

"Two can fit now," Saul called out from inside.

Kann dropped to his knees and crawled inside.

She and Col and Tor continued at a brisker pace to clear away the loose snow shoved out to them.

It would take a while to clear out enough space for all five of them to fit comfortably inside.

EIGHTEEN

NAOMI

They worked steadily for another hour, probably two. Finally, Kann called from inside that they'd reached all the sticks coming through the dome.

The two lion shifters crawled out, Saul was first with his loose golden hair hanging over his shoulders, nearly trailing the snow when he was on all fours. The parka made him look even bulkier than he was.

Kann, bare chested since he'd given his coat to her, followed him out, his hair still neatly arranged down the back of his head.

Tor stood next to Col. Both wore their hair loose, no braids, no decorations. Maybe that was just how it was when they'd left Reylea.

"What is it, *shuarra?*" Col asked, his eyes watching her intently. "I see the question dancing in your mind."

"I—It was silly."

He shook his head. "Ask."

"Your hair, do you always wear it loose?" She gestured to Kann and Saul. "Or do you change it depending on what you're doing?"

Tor chuckled next to Col and followed Kann and Saul up the side of the dome to pull out the large trunk they'd used as a center post.

Col moved closer to Naomi and pulled her to his side. "Do you prefer their hair?" His tone was gruff and laced with just a hint of jealousy.

"No of course not, I was merely curious if it was a tribe thing or a personal style." She threw her arms around his neck.

"Kann's hair is prepared for battle in the style of the Lion Tribe. He is a warrior. Saul's hair would likely look the same if he pulled it up, but he has it loose at the moment, covering the shaved sides. The cords and feathers indicate his rank," Col spoke softly, but not enough so that the others couldn't hear.

"And Tor?"

The tiger shifter leaped down from the dome of the shelter and walked to Col's side. "My people wear their hair loose. No braids." He bowed his head slightly to Col. "The Lion Tribe truly do like to preen and strut. Perhaps it is because their cats are so vain as well."

The tiger jogged off trying to avoid being caught. He was unsuccessful.

"Vain!" Kann leaped at Tor and knocked him to the ground. "Tigers sleep in the trees above the rivers so they can lounge and look at their reflections all day long."

Naomi couldn't help the laughter that bubbled up

from her chest. She covered her mouth and watched the two men wrestle in the snow.

Saul stood to the side, shaking his head, but he too was smiling. For a few moments, the horrors of the last day slipped away.

For a few moments they were just a group of friends goofing off. They reminded her of her brothers. The way they'd fight and argue and dog-pile on top of each other, then when they finally came up for air, they would all be laughing.

It would be nice having them all around. Would feel less like she'd lost her big crazy family. Now, it was looking like she was gaining a new one, complete with crazy protective brothers.

"And you?" she asked, looking back up at her mate.

"Braids are common among our females, but not males," Col answered.

"I don't braid my crazy curls." She ran her fingers through the brown locks hanging just past her ears. "Will that bother you?"

Col gave her a shocked expression. He shook his head. "No, of course not, *shuarra*." He guided her toward the small tunnel entrance to the snow shelter. "Go inside, I will be right behind you."

"What about the others?"

He sighed. "When they get cold enough, they will return."

Naomi knelt down and crawled on all fours through the short tunnel into the center of the igloo-like shelter.

It wasn't an igloo. No ice bricks. Once through the

entrance, the dome rose quite high. She could easily stand up in the center, closest to the vent hole.

Col was right behind her, having just a little more trouble crawling through the small opening.

"Do you want some help," she asked, offering her hand and a teasing smile.

He grumbled and growled and finally shoved his way into the domed area. It was light enough to see, but not too bright inside. "Will a fire not melt the walls?" he asked, running his hands along the inside edges of the dome.

"It supposedly will melt it just enough so that it refreezes into ice and becomes stronger." She sank to the ground and drew her legs up under the coat so only her feet were touching the snow beneath. The coat was long enough to completely cover her, so no one could see beneath it. It was more than a little uncomfortable being completely naked around four men. At least Kann had offered the coat, or she'd just be sitting buck ass naked in front of everyone.

That would be more awkward.

Noise outside made Naomi dip her head to peer out the entrance.

Col moved to stand between her and the noise. She could hear his dragon rumbling and his shoulders were tense.

When Tor's red hair showed through the opening, he relaxed and moved to crouch on the ground next to her.

"We brought firewood." The tiger shifter crawled the rest of the way into the shelter and dropped an armful of snapped branches in the center of the space. "It'll be hard to get a flame started on these big logs, and we couldn't find anything that would work for kindling."

Kann and Saul were right behind him, each carrying an armful of firewood.

"I will light it." Col released a heavy sigh. "Come outside." He gestured to Tor.

He and the tiger shifter crawled back through the tunnel.

Kann and Saul moved to the far side of the open space, away from Naomi and leaned back against the dome wall.

"So how does it feel to be a dragon?" Kann asked, leaning forward so that his elbows rested on his crossed legs.

"I don't really feel that different. I mean. I'm warmer. Stronger. There's this voice sometimes in my head. Almost like it has an opinion and feelings. So, I guess that's strange." Naomi rubbed her chin against the place where her knees were hidden by the parka. "I don't think we've known each other long enough for me to truly have an opinion yet. What about your animals? Do they speak to you?"

"They do not typically speak the way you or I would, but yes, they do use short phrases or words from time to time to convey feelings or urges. Usually when we're doing something they either disagree with, or really like. There's not much middle ground." He chuckled softly.

That information aligned with what Naomi had experienced so far. She focused her attention on the entrance tunnel again.

A bright flame came through first.

Col was holding a large log, flaming on one end and completely charred all the way down. It would've burned anyone else, but her mate was able to carry it as if it were nothing.

He set it down in the center of the mounded firewood and coaxed the flame to catch on several logs before returning to her side.

"Where's Tor?" she asked, watching the tunnel.

"He's on first watch." Col tugged her from the ground onto his lap. "We will take shifts. I do not want to be surprised if the Wolf Tribe comes around again."

Kann and Saul nodded their agreement and scooted closer to the slowly growing campfire in the center of the shelter.

———

COL

"You saw more of the wolves, like the one who attacked me?" His mate curled into his lap and shuddered.

"No one will touch you, Naomi. You are safe with us." Col kept his voice soft and relaxed. The last thing he wanted her to know was that there was a large pack of Wolf Tribe very close to this mountain.

Kann and Saul met his gaze for a moment and nodded, giving him their silent word that they would stick with him.

Col felt a sense of security with the big cats at his side. In Reylea, they would've attacked each other on sight. Here, they were allies. Friends. Even family.

He owed them his loyalty for life.

Perhaps the separation of tribes in Reylea had been a mistake. There'd just never been a reason to change. Everyone had been set in their ways, including his tribe. His family.

Now things were different. Just as his mate had pointed out. They were all that was left of the N'ra Lowland Tribes.

If they didn't work together, they wouldn't survive. If they did, they could thrive. Nothing was stronger and more determined than a Tribe.

Col leaned back against the dome wall. The light from the fire gave the snow tent a warm glow. For being made of snow, it was surprisingly comfortable. The wind outside and the air that burned lungs was the true enemy.

Kann scooted toward the entrance. "I'm going to see if I can scrounge up something to eat."

"Thank you," Naomi said before Col could even open his mouth.

"Thank you, brother," he echoed, using the term of affection again.

The lion shifter tipped his chin respectfully and crawled out of the snow tent.

It'd felt strange the first time to call him *brother*, but now, it felt more and more natural. They were his kindred. His brothers.

These men had risked their lives to help him save his mate.

Nothing had asked them to reach out to him. Naomi

meant nothing to them. She did now. She was part of their tribe and females were important. Treasured.

With Fate's guidance, hopefully their little band would grow, and the other males would soon find their mates as well.

More women in the group would make his *shuarra* pleased. A big family. It would be good for him too.

Col was used to having a large family as well. Fate had known exactly what he needed to push him past the darkness that'd driven him to deliver justice—revenge.

Naomi hadn't been wrong. He had made Jaha suffer. In the end, he'd made Sefa suffer as well. His justice had been mixed with revenge, and it'd been bitter and unsatisfactory.

It was over now.

Now was the time to rebuild. To start fresh with his mate, and his new brothers.

Naomi turned and snuggled closer. Her breathing slowed and within moments she was making a soft snoring sound, her breath warming his chest. Her body warming his heart. He'd never fail her again. Never be distracted by darkness and hate again.

She was his world now.

"Sleep for a while, Col," Saul said from across the space. "You'll heal faster."

Col sighed but did close his eyes. He tightened his hold on Naomi and let himself slip away for a few minutes.

When he opened them again, Saul was gone. Kann was back.

A small animal was roasting over the fire in the center of the room. The smell was mouthwatering.

Tor sat next to Kann.

"He lives," the tiger shifter chuckled.

Col growled, and Naomi patted his chest and shushed him. He looked down at her face. Her heart rate was even. Her breathing was still slow and deep. She was still asleep.

"Even in her sleep your mate knows I'm only teasing you," Tor said.

"It will take time for me to not..." he paused, not sure what he was trying to say.

"Overreact?" Kann interjected. He sliced off a bit of meat and handed it to Col.

"Naomi." Col jostled her gently. "Eat, *shuarra*."

They hadn't eaten last night before everything happened and now it was well into the mid-day, and this was the first opportunity to eat.

He was hungry, but his mate had been through hell. Her body had changed into a dragon. She hadn't fed. She'd be starving.

Naomi stirred in his lap and her brown eyes popped open, flecks of gold swirled in the irises. Her dragon was close, probably nagging and wanting to change again.

"How are you, my mate?"

Her gaze flicked to the strip of meat in his hand and then back to his face. "Is that for me?"

He smiled.

She clambered off his lap carefully and he gave her the morsel. She tore into it quickly and moaned in pleasure.

The other men stared, and Col snarled, sending their wandering eyes back to the fire and the roasting game.

"This is so good. I'm so hungry." Her voice was husky and needy and sounded as if she'd had more than just a good bite of food. "Ohmygod!"

Col tamped down his dragon and tried to will his erection back down. Food should not make his mate so pleased. Only *he* should be able to illicit sounds like that from her body.

Other men should absolutely not hear her pleasure sounds.

"Thank you." Naomi's voice was still barely more than a suggestive moan. "Can I have more?"

Neither Kann nor Tor moved or turned their head. Neither male spoke to or even looked at his mate.

Col had to give them credit for their control.

"Naomi." The word brought her focus to him. Her eyes were half-gold right now. Her heart was racing. He put a hand on her leg and pinned her with his gaze. "You must settle. If you change now, you will destroy the shelter. Breathe slowly and focus on your human body. Two legs. Two arms. Beautiful curly hair."

"You like my hair." Her tone softened and returned to its normal tone.

"I love your hair, *shuarra*." Col stroked his hand up and down her thigh.

"It was so strange. I knew what was going on, but *she* wanted more and was pushing so hard. I couldn't think straight."

He nodded. "It will take time for you to find the balance with your animal. Reyleans are taught to control them from the time they are small children. You have no training and a full-grown dragon."

"So, I could just freak out at any moment and turn into a dragon the size of a single-wide?"

"I don't know what a single-wide is, but yes. Younglings struggle with balance and often have moments where they lose control and turn against their will."

"Not cool," Naomi muttered. "I'm still hungry though. Is there enough for me to have more?"

"You are welcome to as much as you can eat." Tor sliced off another strip and handed it to Col.

"Well, you guys need to eat too," she said.

Col handed her the warm slice of roasted game and smiled. "You eat what you want. We can always get more."

Tor nodded. "Even this high on the mountain, there is plenty to hunt."

"You didn't let anyone see you," Naomi asked.

"I don't—"

"People," Saul's voice hissed through the shelter opening.

"Wolves?" Col moved quickly through the tunnel to Saul's side.

The lion shifter shook his head and pointed toward the bottom of the hillside.

Col recognized the sound of the thing Naomi had made him ride. The *vehicle* she had called it.

The people on the snowmachines were wearing brightly colored coats. It was a big group.

He counted ten people and five snowmachines. His skin prickled and burned.

His dragon wanted to eliminate them.

No people. No threat.

"You can't just get rid of them." Naomi crawled through the tunnel behind him. She climbed to her feet and shoved her way between himself and Saul's body. "I know what you're thinking, barbarian. Hulk smash. But that's not going to work this time."

"I will keep you safe."

"I'll get us off this mountain. They look like people. They smell like people." She sniffed the air.

Col raised an eyebrow in surprise. She could scent like a Reylean too? Though, he shouldn't be surprised. She was a dragon now.

"Are they?" she asked, looking first to him and then to Saul.

"Yes," they both answered.

"Good, then maybe we can get them to drive us down, so we don't have to walk the whole way, cause if you think you're going to get me to fly come this evening, you're wrong, pal." She patted Col's arm. "I might be a dragon, but I'm still terrified of heights."

Saul covered his mouth and held in a muffled laugh.

"Don't laugh at my mate." Col slipped an arm around her waist and flashed a deadly glare at the lion shifter.

"You want to laugh too." Naomi sighed. "Admit it. I can hear it in your voice."

He refused to laugh. It rippled inside him, but he kept it together. He'd never encountered a dragon who was afraid of heights. The idea was absurd.

Dragons were made to be in the sky. They weren't made to flounder about like a lizard on the ground.

She'd overcome her fear. It might take time, but she'd get there.

"Why would they help us? We have nothing to give them? They don't know us," Saul said as the people continued to come closer.

"They look like campers. Ten to one says they've never seen a shelter like the one we just built. We could offer them that in exchange for taking us down to McKinley Park." She took a step forward and waved.

The lead snowmachine changed course and the entire group started toward them.

"Plus, if they end up dangerous, Col can burn them up, right?" Naomi glanced over her shoulder with an expectant look.

Col chuckled. "I will be ready, my *shuarra*."

CHAPTER
NINETEEN

NAOMI

Naomi pulled on the hem of the coat she was wearing. It covered halfway down her thighs, but still, the cold air whipping up under made her uncomfortable.

Not cold, but the people quickly approaching were going to wonder how she wasn't frostbitten and dead. No boots. No pants. No gloves. Just an oversized parka and four oversized dudes.

Okay, maybe they wouldn't wonder how she was staying warm. It was quite possible they would think she was sleeping with all four of the guys.

The day was beautiful and clear. The sky was pure blue. Not a cloud in sight. The sun fell bright and warm on her face, even though the actual temperature was probably close to negative ten or more.

She glanced quickly between Saul and Col.

Saul had a coat on, but Col was of course bare-chested and utterly delicious.

Focus.

Their clothes would also raise a lot of questions. Naomi had no idea how to explain away the two giant Reylean warriors at her side, not to mention the other two still inside the snow shelter.

The group of sleds stopped about twenty feet away and two people got off the front one. A guy and a girl.

At least they aren't all men.

Their bright clothing meant they weren't hunters. No white coveralls to hide themselves from sight in the snow. Also meant they were very likely to be tourists. Most of the locals she'd noticed wore gear that blended more into the landscape. Black and brown.

"Hey," one of the approaching guys called out. He was tall, maybe six feet. Burly, but not nearly as big as Col or Saul. "What...who are you guys?" He gazed up and down her body and then turned his attention to Col and Saul.

"We got stranded out here." Naomi took a leap of faith and just dove in. "We could really use a ride down to McKinley Park."

"What happened to your snowmachines? How did you get out here?" The woman next to him asked. She was about Naomi's size, with long blonde hair sticking out of her knitted hat.

"The people we were with took them and left us here. It was supposed to be a social experiment, but it's been a nightmare," Naomi said, finally landing on a plausible story. "We could really use the help."

"We can call the park service. I'm sure they'd come get you," the guy said.

"We're really trying to keep all of this out of the papers," she continued. The last thing she needed was authorities asking the guys for their non-existent IDs.

"Is that an igloo?" the woman asked, leaning to the side to get a better look around Saul's body. "So cool. How did you guys make that? How big is it?"

"Pretty big. We've got a campfire inside and everything."

"So, this social experiment. Is that why you guys don't have enough clothes on? How are you not freezing?" the woman asked, directing her attention back to Naomi.

"Yeah. Bad joke gone really wrong. I've got a lot to report back at work when I finally get off this mountain. Where is your group from?"

"Oh, we're all from California. Can I go in your igloo?"

"Tell you what," Naomi started, "If a few of you guys can spare a couple hours to give us a ride back to McKinley Park, the campsite is yours. There're only five of us."

"Two more?" the dude asked, looking around.

"Do they look like these two? Can they talk? Or do they just stand there and look yummy?" the woman asked, letting her eyes rove over Col and then Saul.

"Barbara!" the guy next to her snapped. "Seriously."

"Well, they do look like they just walked off the set of a fantasy movie," she said, giving puppy dog eyes to her companion.

Naomi felt her dragon growl. *Mine.* She coughed to

cover the sound and patted her chest, pretending to have choked ... on air. Whatever. As long as she didn't go dragon-woman on this chick's ass for checking out her mate.

Col slipped an arm around her waist and pulled her close. "We would appreciate the help. Tor. Kann," Col called. His voice soothed her dragon. His touch probably even more so.

The other two warriors crawled out of the shelter to stand next to them.

Naomi took a deep breath.

They were quite the crazy looking group.

"Holy crap," the woman said, her tone rising. "They really do *all* look like that."

"So, we take you down the mountain and we get your campsite and the igloo?"

"With our gratitude," Saul said from his place standing to Naomi's right. "We also have most of a deer roasting inside that you are welcome to."

"I knew something smelled delicious. Jeff, we have to do this. We will get to tell our friends we stayed in a real igloo. Think of the pictures!" The blonde woman practically squealed with excitement. "We have more than enough sleds. It'll only take about an hour or so to get them over the river."

The guy—apparently Jeff—nodded. "Sure. Let me talk to the others. Works for me though."

THE RIDE WAS UNEVENTFUL. For once, something went smoothly. No shifting. No dragons swooping out of the air to snatch her away. No wolves tried to kill her. It really was an improvement.

The sky was bright, and the snow was crisp. If it wasn't for the fact Naomi was riding on a snowmachine going eighty miles an hour and naked except for a coat, sitting behind a chick named Barbara she'd only just met, it would be perfect.

When Col had realized they would all have to ride with someone from the other group, he'd been upset.

Scratch that. Upset was an understatement.

She'd had to beg him to control himself when one of the guys offered her a ride. When she explained her circumstance—the no underwear—to Barbara, the nice woman had offered to drive the last sled instead of her *male* cohort.

Col had been appeased by this option and they were now approaching the bridge over the river to the resorts in McKinley Park.

Naomi couldn't wait to get into one of the shops and get some clothes. Once all the guys looked like they were from *this* world, they could get back up to the cabin she'd rented and figure out the next step from there.

Her mom and sister were probably freaking out again, since she'd for sure gone longer than twenty-four hours without calling. Again.

The snowmachine slowed.

She took a breath and loosened the hold she had around Barbara's waist. The other sleds slowed as well and a moment later they were at a complete stop.

"Which resort?" Barbara asked.

"The McKinley Chalet," Naomi responded. She'd shopped in a store right down the road from the resort before she headed out to Curtis' cabin. It would be the best option for finding the men something appropriate to wear for the winter weather.

The blonde nodded and motioned for the rest of the entourage to follow her across the Nenana River Bridge and into the resort area.

The motors on the sleds roared to life one at a time and soon they were racing down the ice and snow-covered road toward McKinley Park and its wide assortment of cabins and resorts and hotels.

Everyone from serious climbers to families of four came through McKinley Park to visit Denali National Park.

The red-roofed Swiss-chalet-style resort was connected by snow-covered boardwalks to several shops and restaurants, all tucked between fragrant spruce trees. Standing in front of the building itself, it gave the illusion of being the only place for miles. Smart designer.

When in fact there were several other resort hotels, shopping, and cabins just a few miles down the road and an airport not much further south of those.

The group stopped in front of the Chalet.

Naomi, Col, and the others climbed off the sleds.

"You sure you're going to be okay?" Barbara asked, pulling off her goggles.

She smiled. "Yes, thank you. We really appreciate your help. It would've been a really long walk."

"Girl, you would've lost toes and fingers if you'd tried

to walk that back." The blonde shook her head. "Okay, well, as long as you're good from here. We've got to get back. Can't have the group climbing up Denali without us."

"Thanks for the campsite," one of the guys at the back of the line shouted.

Naomi waved.

Col and the others stood quietly behind her.

When she turned, they were staring in awe—and maybe a little hesitation—at the huge hotel ahead of them.

A few people were out walking the boardwalks, and her mate's bare chest and eight pack abs were definitely drawing attention.

Kann's too, since he'd given her the parka to wear.

Her bare legs and feet probably weren't helping either.

"We've got to get to a phone. I need money and all my stuff is up at the cabin."

"Is this where your king lives?" Kann asked.

Naomi sputtered and coughed and turned away from the guys until she could control her reaction.

Col stroked her back so sweetly. As if worried something was actually wrong.

"No, no king. This is a hotel. People stay here temporarily to hike and explore the mountain range. Like me. Remember, I said I didn't live here. I paid for the cabin for seven days. Then I was going back to New York."

"You are not leaving now?" Col asked, with just the slightest bit of hesitancy.

She shook her head and stood up straight, taking in a deep breath. "No, Col, I'm not leaving." Naomi leaned against his side and breathed in his masculine scent.

His arm encircled her body and squeezed gently.

"My family is going to freak out when they hear I'm staying in Alaska ... well, my sister might not be surprised, but my brothers are going to lose their minds." She peered up at him.

He was smiling. "Older brothers?"

"Yes," she answered. "Two."

"Is your sister coming here?" Kann asked.

Naomi turned and narrowed her gaze at Kann. "No," she said. "Don't get any ideas."

He shrugged. "You are an excellent mate. It would be logical to assume another female in your family could be—"

"No," Naomi said again, more forcefully this time.

The lion shifter snapped his mouth shut and nodded, but she figured the whole looking-for-a-mate mentality wouldn't disappear for long.

"All right guys, time to find you some clothes that will help you blend in a bit better." She pointed toward the small cabin-ish building at the end of the board walk—Denali Mountain Works. She walked through the sludgy mess of snow and ice, trying to find good footing. Before she'd taken two steps, Col lifted her off the ground.

"You should not be walking in this. The ground is so cold it burns like fire," he said, stealing a quick kiss.

"At least you have boots on," she replied.

He grunted. "They are not made for this climate."

"Nothing we are wearing is made for this climate," Tor muttered from behind them, clomping through the snow on the road up to the cleared paths on the boardwalk.

"So, this entire place is for visitors?" Col asked, staring up and down the massive boardwalk at the resort hotel and surrounding buildings.

Some were private cabins. Some were restaurants. Naomi had stayed at the Chalet one night before heading up to the cabin she'd rented.

"No one lives here?"

"People live in the area, but not in that building. That's a hotel. Just visitors," she said. "We need that door." She pointed again to the log cabin shop.

Col nodded and redirected.

Tor reached the entrance first. "Do we request permission to enter?" the tiger asked, looking back at Naomi.

She shook her head. "It's a store. Just pull the door open and go in."

He did as she'd directed, and soon they were in the cozy little cabin. Surrounded by clothes and snow gear and cute little souvenirs.

There were even some hunting knives on display right at the front.

Kann and Saul both moved to study them more closely.

A woman about Naomi's age stood behind the counter in stunned silence.

She patted Col's arm and he put her down gently. Once her feet touched the floor, she yanked on the coat she was wearing to make sure it covered all the important bits.

"Hey." Naomi approached the counter. She pushed Kann and Tor out of the way.

Both males vacated the space in front of the counter quickly to give her space.

"So, I need to make a quick phone call to my sister in New York. I don't have my wallet with me; it's up at the cabin I was staying at. As you can see, my friends and I are not dressed for the weather. Office prank gone horribly wrong." She paused, giving the round-faced brunette a moment to process. "Can I borrow your cell phone for just a sec? My sister will pay for everything we need over the phone if that's okay?"

The woman's blue eyes turned to her and slowly started to focus. "Are you naked?"

Naomi chuckled. "Yes."

"Ohmygod, how are you not dead? It was thirty below last night."

"Luck and these big guys behind me." She gave a knowing wink at the woman.

The store clerk's cheeks flushed a bright pink and she smiled. "Is there some kind of movie being filmed nearby?"

Naomi considered the question and then nodded. "I can't talk about it though, sorry. But I really did get separated from my ID and wallet. Do you have a cell?"

"Oh, yeah. No problem," the woman answered, pulling a cellphone from her back pocket. "Do they need help?" She pointed, and Naomi turned to see Kann and Tor sniffing the racks of clothes.

She inwardly rolled her eyes and sighed. Col was still standing right behind her. As was Saul. She could hear and smell them both, even though they were out of her line of sight.

"They will need so much help," she muttered, unable to hold back a slight chuckle.

"I'd be happy to show them *anything*," the clerk said, "I'm Jess, by the way."

"Naomi," she answered, taking the offered cell phone. "They won't know what size they wear or anything. Foreigners." Naomi started to type in her sister's phone number.

Please be around.

"Do they speak English?" Jess asked, walking around the counter and heading toward Kann and Tor.

Naomi nodded and put the phone to her ear. "Yes, they do." She turned to Col and Saul. "Go with her."

Col shook his head, but the lion shifter accepted the instruction and moved stealthily behind poor Jess.

When the clerk turned to ask Naomi another question she nearly collided with Saul's massive body.

"Oh, I'm so sorry," the woman squeaked. "What exactly do you all need?" she called out from around Saul's body.

"Cam?" Naomi said into the phone microphone.

"Yeah?" her sister answered. *"What's going on? Whose phone are you on?"*

"Hang on a second." She took a step and looked around Col's chest. "They each need a full set of clothes and a set of snow pants or overalls to go on over that. They also need a winter coat, gloves, hat, and boots."

"You got it!" Jess hollered back, giving Naomi a salute and a wide smile.

She grinned and watched as the young woman started ordering around the big warriors.

They did everything she asked and watched her every move.

Naomi was secretly glad Col had refused to leave her side. She would've been jealous if Jess was staring at him the way she was the other three.

"Cam, I got separated from my wallet. It's back at the cabin, but I've got to get clothes for the guys, so they can get me back up there. I need you to pay for everything with your credit card. I'll PayPal you the money the second I get back to the cabin and my laptop."

"*Guys?*" Suspicion colored her sister's voice. "*Where's Col? I thought he was from there. Why wouldn't he have clothes?*"

"Long story, will have to tell you later. Can we please call you back in like thirty minutes and get you to pay for the supplies?"

"*Yeah, that's fine, but I expect an explanation at some point. You do realize that, right?*"

"I do."

"*I'll tell Mama and Papa and the boys not to worry ... or, should they be worried?*" Cam asked.

"I'm fine. I promise. I'm just going to make some pretty significant life changes over the next week or so," Naomi said nonchalantly, hoping her sister wouldn't completely lose her shit.

It was a pipe dream though.

"*Nai! You did marry the guy, didn't you?*"

"I-uh—"

"Nai!"

"Sorta, yeah. I'm moving to Alaska."

"Holy shit! Mama's gonna have a heart attack. Are you sure?"

"I'm really sure, Cam. I'm so happy with Col. This is really good."

Col nuzzled her neck and his chest purred—hummed —and Naomi smiled.

"Tell Mama and Papa it's good. I'll call you back in a few minutes. We have to get some winter gear. And when I get back to the cabin, I'll Skype you again, okay?"

"Yeah, yeah, no problem. I'll keep the phone right here next to me," Cam said.

"Thanks, Cam, love you," Naomi said.

"Love you too, little sis," Cam answered before Naomi hung up the line and put the phone down on the counter.

She turned to Col. "Time to get us some clothes too."

CHAPTER
TWENTY

COL

Col stared at himself in the reflecting glass Naomi had called a *mirror*. It was like someone had captured the clearness of the water's surface and locked it into a rock.

He'd never seen something that looked so perfect. He touched his finger to the mirror in the dressing room again and shook his head.

Uncanny.

The clothing was strange. Heavy. Warm.

Naomi had assured him he was more than welcome to change back into his *tosa*—or kilt as she called it—once they were back at the cabin and out of the public eye.

If these clothes pleased his mate, he'd learn to wear them. He was on earth now, not Reylea.

The boots were thick and warm, much better for treading through the deep snow and ice than his thinner, softer leather ones. The shirt was red and white and orange in a pattern Naomi called *plaid.*

It'd taken him ages to get the small buttons on the front aligned and connected correctly.

He pushed open the dressing room door and peered out.

Naomi was standing next to Tor, Kann, and Saul. They were all dressed like him, with different colored shirts. Big heavy black boots and puffy black snow pants on over what Naomi called *jeans.* Personally, he thought they were rather constricting.

His mate smiled and clapped her hands excitedly. She was in a new pair of *jeans* and a dark purple shirt he'd insisted on after seeing it on the wall.

She looked delectable. The jeans clung to every curve. He wanted to strip her out of everything the second he got her alone again.

A pair of dark blue snow pants hung over her arm, along with a pair of boots she hadn't put on yet. The woman from the shop stood a little to his right.

"Good fit," she said.

"Excellent," Naomi said. "Gloves, hats, and everything else are on the counter already, along with duffle bags for you guys to carry your stuff in." She handed a small black square to the other woman—a cellphone—and motioned for him and the others to follow her back to the front counter. She sat down and wiggled into her snow pants. Then shoved on her boots.

He waited at her side until she was done lacing everything up.

"It's weird not really needing these clothes." Naomi kept her voice soft.

Tor and the lions were at the counter laughing with the clerk about something. All three men had been enamored with the woman, and she with them.

"It is as you said ... better to not draw attention to ourselves by wearing what is expected. Your inner body heat will adjust. You won't be uncomfortable." Col offered his hand and she smiled up at him as she took it. He pulled her up from the chair and tugged her close to his side. "I will enjoy peeling every layer off of you later tonight." His voice dropped to a growl, pleased with the pink flush that crept up into her cheeks.

She smiled coyly.

The woman at the counter motioned for her to come, and Naomi gave him a quick wink before wriggling away to tend to whatever needed to be done to pay for their clothing and *gear* as she called it.

"Thank you so much, sis." Naomi directed her voice at the cellphone. "I'll talk to you tonight, once I get back to the cabin."

"*Sounds good, Nai. I gotta run. You going to be good after this?*"

"Yep," she answered.

The clerk put the phone down and handed his mate a long strip of white material. "Here's your receipt. If something doesn't work correctly, you have thirty days to come exchange it for a different size or brand."

"Great, thank you so much for your help. I know we tore apart your shop trying to find everything the guys needed."

"Not a problem." The woman smiled up at Tor the whole time. "If you need anything else, just let me know."

Col shook his head.

The woman was obviously interested in the tiger shifter, but Tor was barely paying attention and playing with something on the bag Naomi had picked out for him.

Col grabbed the blue bag from the counter that had his *tosa* and other belongings in it and slung it over his shoulder.

The three men followed suit, each thanking the shop keeper for her help.

Tor moved a few steps ahead of their group and held open the door.

They stepped out onto the boardwalk. The sky was clear, and the sun was shining.

The crisp refreshing smell of the surrounding forests filled Col's lungs. He couldn't wait to see the countryside when it wasn't blanketed by snow and ice.

"Mr. Curtis," Naomi called out and waved at a man down near the road.

He was wearing a bright blue hat and a big brown coat. He stood near what Col now knew was called a *car*.

The vehicle was black and had four wheels and four doors.

"Ah, Ms. Parker," he called back, waving her over.

They approached the man who Naomi was renting her cabin from.

The stranger gave Col a once over and then took his time looking over the other three men as well. "You collected yourself some friends?"

"I did," his mate said, laughing lightly. "Thank you so much for finding a place for them. I know it was very last minute."

"Of course, it's a bit rough, but if they don't mind doing the repairs, it would help me out for next season to have another functioning cabin. I just don't have the time myself to put into it."

"We would be happy to put any work into the cabin you wish, Mr. Curtis." Saul stepped forward. "Thank you for your generosity."

The older man nodded. "You're very welcome, boys. You sure you're going to be okay, all of you staying there together? It's a big cabin, but old."

"We will make it work," Naomi said quickly.

"Fair 'nough," Mr. Curtis answered. He opened the door on the back of his vehicle and gestured to them. "Put your bags in the back. I'll get you out to the cabin you've got for another week, Ms. Parker. And then I'll show you boys the trail that'll take you right over to the other one."

"Your help is most appreciated, Mr. Curtis."

Col's mate was incredible. She was upending her entire life to stay here with him. Hell, she wasn't even mad that she'd been turned into a dragon. Despite not knowing that would happen, he couldn't say he wasn't pleased, but she was terrified of flying and clumsy in her full-grown dragon form. So, it would be slow going for a while to get her adjusted to sharing a body with the spirit of an animal.

On top of being *his* mate, she was helping the entire group find a place to live and work.

THE DRIVE to the cabin took about three hours. The conversation was mostly Mr. Curtis, telling them all the things that needed to be fixed in the cabin he was going to let them stay in and how he dreamed of having even more cabins to have enough steady income to retire soon.

Col watched the landscape out the window of the vehicle, trying to memorize positions and placements so he wouldn't get lost if they needed to come south to this place again—McKinley Park.

"You know it's not much, but Mystery is a great town to live in. It's not big, but there's a mechanic and gas station, a diner, a post office..." The man's voice trailed off. "Several water pump stations, and a small grocer slash hardware store. If you need something specific, it's likely that the Jenkins' can get it ordered in for you. There's a landing strip just outside of town too and they have a good relationship with lots of wholesalers down at the coast."

"It's going to be an adventure." His mate leaned against him.

They were in the back seat of the van.

Kann and Saul were in the middle.

Tor had taken the front seat next to Mr. Curtis.

Col nodded and kissed the top of Naomi's head. He slipped an arm around her shoulders and pulled her even closer. "You are my adventure."

"I like the sound of that. You know I'm still not going to fly with you." She kept her voice low so no one else would hear.

"Give it time, *shuarra*. Eventually you will be comfortable."

The van stopped, and he looked up.

They were back at the cabin.

"Do you want to see the other cabin? The bigger one where you'll all be staying?" Mr. Curtis asked from the driver's seat.

"I need to call my sister before it's too late tonight in New York, so show them everything, and if you wouldn't mind writing down a list for me so I can keep track. That would really help." She leaned in the window where Tor was sitting.

Col felt his dragon flex and growl. She was too close to the tiger. Even though his brain knew she wasn't the least bit interested in Tor, instinct didn't want her anywhere near an unmated male. If Tor had a mate, it'd be a different story, but he didn't. Therefore, Tor was a threat.

"Of course, Ms. Parker," Mr. Curtis said. "Will do."

"Wait." He growled and climbed from his seat. Col got out of the van and joined Naomi. "I need to check the cabin. Make sure she's safe before we go."

Mr. Curtis gave him an approving nod and waved them on.

"I'll be okay, Col."

"And I will be satisfied after I've checked the cabin and made sure you are safe." he answered, following her up the steps to the door.

She opened the lock box first with the code, retrieved the key and then opened the door. They stepped into a dark room. Naomi flipped a switch near the door and the light in the center of the ceiling burst to life, illuminating the living area. "Go check," she urged. "I'm getting on my laptop." She walked a few steps to the right and sat at the desk. Opened her device and began typing.

Col took a deep breath. No unfamiliar scents. He checked the washroom and the bedroom in the back before returning to her at the desk. "I will return shortly. Do not leave the cabin until I get back."

"What about the outhouse?"

He growled, remembering her close call with the Wolf Tribe at the other cabin. Still, he couldn't expect her to never walk outside without him again. She was a dragon now. If something happened, her animal's instincts would take over, although Naomi probably didn't know that yet.

"Well?" she asked and peered up at him with a coy smile.

She was testing him. Sneaky mate.

He ruffled her hair and shook his head. "Just be careful if you do. Scent for anything as soon as you open the door and keep your eyes and ears open. Your dragon will help you if you let her."

"Sounds good," Naomi answered. She puckered her lips and closed her eyes, waiting for a kiss.

One he very much wanted to give her. He captured her mouth and tasted her sweetness. She was warm now —like him—but soft and sweet. Col would never tire of touching and tasting and loving her as long as he lived.

She moaned, and he reached for one of her breasts, cupping it and mixing his groan of need with hers.

Naomi was the first to pull away. Her lips were pink and swollen, and her cheeks flushed.

He could smell her arousal in the air.

"You need to go," she said. "They're waiting."

His displeasure rumbled through the quiet space.

"I'll be here when you get back."

"Very well." Col sighed, then walked to the door. He looked back at her once more before stepping out. Beautiful curls. Smiling face. He'd turned her into a dragon, and she still loved him. Still wanted to be with him. His heart swelled in his chest and for just a moment his vision blurred. He blinked it away.

Naomi glanced over her shoulder and met his gaze. For a second, she paused, the excitement in her expression changed to one of adoration. Love. Understanding. Something more than he could have ever hoped for. Dreamed for. Definitely more than he deserved.

She mouthed the words *I love you.*

He mouthed them back. Her face lit up. Her eyes sparkled with flecks of gold he was only just beginning to get used to seeing. She waved and turned back to the computer.

He watched a moment longer. She was putting in her earbuds and bringing up the *Skype* app to speak with her sister. Or mother. Or brothers. He'd lost count of how many people loved her. How could they not? Everyone that met Naomi loved her.

Stay. His dragon growled, but he needed to do his part. They were a tribe now.

He and Tor and Kann and Saul and Naomi. More if they could find them. But right now, this job and the larger cabin Mr. Curtis said they could fix up to live in was their start. His mate was depending on him to make sure this worked out for them. She was giving up her home. Her family.

She'd chosen him.

And he would choose her back every single day of his life.

Thank you for reading *Knock Down Dragon Out*! I hope you enjoyed Col and Naomi's story.

Next up for the Soulmate Shifters is *I'm Not Lion to You*!

In Alaska, lion shifter Kann is on the prowl for his mate, and when he sees Penny, he knows she's the one. She can't deny their powerful attraction, but she fears her past will only hurt their future. Can he persuade her to submit to her desires?

Pick up your copy of ***I'm Not Lion to You*** today!

Subscribe to my VIP Newsletter and get access to ***Fires of Reylea!*** Find out more about how Col got to Alaska! www.krystalshannan.com/newsletter/knock-down-dragon-out-bonus-offer

NEXT UP FOR THE SOULMATE SHIFTERS...

Read a short excerpt below

CHAPTER ONE
PENNY

Penny Matheson climbed out onto the wing of the small plane that had carried her away from Anchorage. Away from the scene of a murder—an execution—that she shouldn't have ever seen.

But she had.

Now she had to deal with it.

Her breath clouded in front of her. The February sky was clear and blue, with no clouds in sight, and the snow on the surrounding hilly landscape was crisp and clean. Worry prickled at the back of her neck like needles from an acupuncture session. She knew she was safe for the moment, but she couldn't help but watch … as if at any moment another plane would appear.

She wouldn't put it past Jake Vicenti to send someone after her … or come himself. But she'd worked hard to disappear. Mystery was barely a dot on the map. No ticket needed for a small plane. No credit card or a cell phone for her boss to track.

Penny stepped from the wing to the razor-narrow metal ledge, avoiding the flap of the wing on her way down to the tarmac. The tall burly pilot came around from the other side and smiled at her the way she imagined a dad would. He had short salt and pepper hair and lines around his mouth that spoke to years of smiles. It was why she'd approached him in Anchorage.

"You're not going to tell anyone you brought me here, right?" She shoved her bare hands into her pockets and breathed slowly. The air was like ice in her lungs. In her hurry to escape, she'd forgotten gloves and a hat. *Stupid.*

"Brought who?" His mouth turned down, like he wanted to ask a question but was second guessing himself. "I just deliver groceries and hardware to the Jenkins."

"Thanks."

"Where's your ride?"

"It's not that far, is it?" Normally, she would've researched everything before making a single move, but she'd just run. There hadn't been time for more. She certainly didn't have a ride.

"You can't *walk* to town. It's damn near twenty below out here. You'd be dead before you made it the first mile. You're already as blue as a sheet of ice on the bay."

"Is it that far?" She hated being a burden, even if Carl didn't seem to mind.

"Yep, too far. Come on." He gestured toward a parked white box truck. "I'll drive you in."

She looked at the road. The wind this far north of the ocean bit way worse here than it did in Anchorage. He was right. She had no business walking and shouldn't have even considered it an option.

The familiar smell of salt in the air had been replaced by the scent of spruce, because instead of an ocean, there was just a sea of snow and trees. It wasn't unpleasant ... just different. The same familiar mountains lay in the distance, except now she was on the north side of the Denali National Park instead of looking up from the south.

"You comin'?" he called out from ahead of her a few yards.

"Yes, thank you." She forced her feet to move forward. Only hours ago, her life had been normal. She'd had a great job at Vicenti Inc, as one of the lead weapons research developers in the world. She'd had a great boss. Jake had been all smile and charm.

Except it'd been a lie.

Today she'd seen Jake, suave debonair professional businessman, kill people. She shuddered a little, remembering the bloody scene that had made her flee Anchorage during her lunch break. Her heart did a little flip-flop and her stomach threatened to vacate its contents.

Vicenti *used* their guns. She'd been developing weapons for criminals.

She took a calming breath and swallowed down her nerves. Jake was barely realizing she'd left by now, and he couldn't possibly have followed her. She'd watched carefully for tails. Watched for anyone.

Her teeth chattered as she climbed into the cab of Carl's delivery truck. He finished loading the boxes from the plane into the back and then climbed into the cab next to her.

"Dammit, girl. You're already freezing, aren't you?" he asked, peeling off his gloves and hat.

"I—can't—"

"You put those on for right now. I know you don't want to talk to me about what's *really* going on or what you're hiding from, but if you freeze to death, it'll all be for nothing, and I won't be able to live with myself, especially since it was me that brought you to this tiny slip of a town."

Her chest tightened, and her eyes welled with unshed tears. "Friends call me Penny." She pulled on his gloves and tugged the Sherpa-lined hat onto her head. Everything smelled like peppermint and gunpowder. The latter might not have comforted a typical person, but the scent of gunpowder made Penny feel safe. That burning bite in her nostrils after firing a gun on the range made her pulse race and adrenaline spread through her system like someone had injected her with superpowers. "Thank you."

"You're right welcome, Penny. You got enough money for a place to stay? Food?"

She nodded. "Yes, I do. I'll be okay. Thank you."

He leaned over a bit and pulled something from his pocket. Penny's eyes widened at the sight of the wad of cash she'd paid him for her seat on his plane. "You take this back. I was coming to Mystery anyway, and having company on the plane was a treat."

"I didn't really talk to you." She didn't take the money. Which was dumb. She needed every dollar she had. There wouldn't be any more, not for a long time. Growing up as a foster kid, though, she'd learned people usually want things in return for doing nice things, especially when related to money.

He shoved it at her chest instead and chuckled. "No, but you were a good listener."

"That's it?"

"That's it." His voice was light and warm and jovial, reminding her of getting a hug from Santa that one year at the mall when she was nine.

Her fingers curled around the precious bills. Having it back would make getting started in town a lot easier. "Thank you." Tears pooled in her eyes again. She sniffed and wiped the corners before they could trail down her cheeks.

Carl nodded, keeping an eye on the road. He pointed to her right as they passed a building with a few cars in the parking lot. "That's the community center. They've got meals every night just in case you find yourself strapped for cash."

Which was very likely. She made a mental note of where the building was.

They went a bit further down the road. Rolling hills covered with trees and snow. More turn offs, and more houses were scattered closer together now. "That's one of the B&B's in town. There's a place with some cabins up the road a bit further, owned by a local, he's also got a few close to town and a few more on the other side of the river. Douglas Curtis is a good guy. He'll give you a fair price and not the tourist price if you tell him I sent you."

The truck continued past a small red building that said groceries and liquor. "Better store is the Jenkins place around the corner. They run the hardware and grocer where most of the town shops. Plus, those in-town cabins of Doug's I was talking about are a quick walk across the street."

"I don't know how to thank you." Penny's voice caught in her throat as all her emotions swirled like snowflakes in the wind. She always tried to plan everything in advance. She hadn't been able to, and it'd been eating away at her during the whole ride. Control was something she'd fought for her entire life. She'd finally gotten some in college and then with her job ... and now it was like being back in the system. Everything was a mess. Everything was uncontrollable.

The older man cursed under his breath. "I'm going to talk to Doug myself." He turned the truck into a small parking lot. The sign on the building said Jenkins Grocery & Hardware. "Why don't you go grab a couple things to help get you started?" He tipped his head across the street, and she followed his gaze to a red building with a sign over it that said Red Bird Cabins for Rent. "I'm only in town for today, but I want to make sure you're set up good, okay."

She nodded. "Thank you. Really."

End of Sample
To continue reading, be sure to pick up *I'm Not Lion to You* at your favorite retailer.

Also by Krystal Shannan

FOR A FULL LIST PLEASE GO TO KRYSTALSHANNAN.COM/BOOKS

Sanctuary, Texas

Paranormal Romance

Completed Series

Sanctuary, Texas will take you on a heart-pounding-toe-curling ride into a town of fantastical creatures and a war for world domination you won't soon forget. The series has fated mates, growly heroes with soft spots for their strong spunky heroines, and enough spicy romance to make you blush. Don't miss this sexy, gritty, paranormal fantasy romance with a twist of darkness. There's a "big bad" you will love to hate and an amazing cast of characters across the series that build a family you won't want to leave behind.

Soulmate Shifters in Mystery, Alaska

Paranormal Shifter Romance

Winter in Mystery, Alaska just got a whole lot hotter. Dragon shifters, lions, and tigers oh my! When the Reylean's world burns, the Tribal survivors find themselves transported to earth through a magickal portal. This series has fated mates, and alpha heroes that will do anything to protect and pleasure and love their women. Come with them on a journey of fitting in, building a new Tribe, and finding out that true family is about more than bloodlines.

VonBrandt Wolf Pack

Paranormal Shifter Romance

Interested in tall, dark, and sexy cowboy wolf shifters? Somewhere, Texas is your town. The VonBrandt Wolf Pack will check every box for you--Stetson-wearing ranchers who can shift into wolves, Fated Mates, and enough high-adrenaline-action to make Bruce Willis shout with glee. Join the VonBrandt men as they win the hearts of the women they love and build a family that will give you all the warm and fuzzies.

Moonbound Wolves

Paranormal Shifter Romance

Completed Series

High octane action builds in this sexy wolf shifter series! A spin-off from the VonBrandt Wolf Pack Series. Follow the enforcers from the Somewhere, TX wolf pack as they uncover a sinister evil that threatens magick as they know it. Each of the seven books offers a happily ever after for a fated mate pair and will propel you into the next leg of the group's across-the-globe mission. Sexy cowboy werewolves and the mates they can't live without, meddling witches, and conspiracies abound in this action-packed paranormal romance series you won't want to miss.

Vegas Mates

Paranormal Shifter Romance

Completed Series

A high-paced series with fated wolf mates fighting to save the people they love. Jump on this roller coaster with sexy shifter men who will go through any trial and women who will stand at their side fangs bared. Follow the Demakis shifter sisters on their journey through their past and how it's affecting their future. Along the way they discover there's so much more to the legends about their wolves than their parents ever let on.

Bad Boys, Billionaires & Bachelors

Contemporary Romance

Completed Series

These three billionaire brothers from small-town Somewhere, TX will warm your hearts and make your toes curl all on the same page. The Stinson men are in a pickle. Good old grandpa put a clause in the will that says they can't inherit the family railroad business unless they get married and have a baby on the way in less than a year. Laugh and cry your way through their antics as they try to figure out how to open their hearts and their homes to women that take them totally by surprise! The sexy and emotional romps continue with more Somewhere, TX bachelors and bad boys!

ABOUT THE AUTHOR

Krystal Shannan, a *USA Today* bestselling author, spins tales of fate and family, weaving her unique brand of magick, fantasy, and passion into captivating stories that pull you into another world. Nestled in her spacious ranch-style home in the heart of Texas with her husband of twenty years, teenage children, and surrounded by a beloved menagerie of animals, her life mirrors the core themes of her work – love, laughter, and a warm sense of home.

Her narratives are a delightful blend of the enchanting and the relatable, marked by vibrant characters, rich world-building, and an emotional depth that resonates with her readers. Her books are filled with humor that tickles your funny bone and romantic undertones that promise to tug at your heartstrings.

Krystal's talent for crafting love stories with a twist of fantasy and a touch of suspense has not only earned her a loyal following but also established her as a stand-out author in the paranormal romance genre. She brings to life relatable characters navigating their destinies, and couples whose passionate connections you can't help but madly and deeply fall for.

So, if you're in the mood to delve into a world where anything is possible, where humor, heartwarming romance, and adventure intertwine, pick up one of Krystal's books. Prepare to be swept away by narratives that not only transport you to magical realms but also remind you of the enduring power of fate and the forever bond of family.

Krystal Shannan is represented by Cole Lanahan from the **Seymour Agency**.

You can find Krystal at www.krystalshannan.com.

amazon.com/author/krystalshannan

bookbub.com/authors/krystal-shannan

goodreads.com/KrystalShannan

facebook.com/KrystalShannan

tiktok.com/@krystalshannan

Made in United States
North Haven, CT
03 June 2024

53281339R00152